I Bear Witness

By Amani-Nzinga Jabbar

ISBN: 9798640692808
Imprint: Independently published

Any references to historical events, real people, or real places are used fictitiously. Names, characters, and places are products of the author's imagination.

First printing edition 2020.

This book is dedicated to my family.

Thank you Ummi and Abu for always being there.

Thank you to Tajuddeen, Zakiyyah and Zuri for being patient with my hours of writing.

Thank you to Umar for your encouragement.

O ye who believe! seek help with patient perseverance and prayer; for
Allah is with those who patiently persevere. [Qur'an[1] 2:153]

'Is the reward for good anything but good?'

There are seven types of people whom Allah[2] will shade on The Day of Judgement. I have known this list for so long, that I can't remember a time when I did not know it. I can't recall the first time I heard it, but it was probably in one of my father's khutbahs[3], or maybe I

---

[1] The Qur'an is the Islamic Holy Book.
[2] Allah is the Arabic word for God.

picked it up from my mother, who would often speak using hadiths as a means to emphasize her words. The seven types of people who earn Allah's shade are the just ruler, someone who grows up worshipping their lord, a person whose heart is attached to the masjid[4], two people who love each other for God's sake, a man who is called by a woman and replies "I fear Allah," a person who gives in charity and conceals it, and a person who remembers Allah in solitude and his eyes fill with tears.

When I was old enough to truly understand the meaning of this saying, I was sure that Allah would shade me fully on the Day of Judgement. Not only was my heart attached to the masjid, my soul, spirit and physical body were as well. The masjid was as much a part of me as the color of my eyes or the shade of my skin. The masjid has always been a place of comfort and serenity for me, since I was a young child.

My earliest memories do not take place in my childhood home, instead they take place in the tiny kitchen of Masjidul-Ihsan. I remember pulling myself up by my mother's dark green apron, her picking me up and holding me on her hip as she prepared one of the many community dinners she was known for. I was often by my mother's side in the masjid kitchen. I

---

[3] Sermons.
[4] Masjid is the Arabic term for Mosque, the Islamic place of worship.

would watch intently as she would add ingredients to various pots and pans. I watched as she tasted dishes and adjusted seasonings. I watched as she checked pies and cakes for doneness with wooden toothpicks. I observed it all.

When I was very young, it seemed mysterious magic to me the way she could turn flour, eggs, and beans into delicious pies. Some of which, she would wrap and sell. My father once got stickers created for her: *From Malikah's Masjid Kitchen.* She would attach these stickers to her bean pies and other desserts which were sold on a table after Friday prayers.

My mother kept a box filled with index cards, on which she had written all of her recipes in her neat cursive handwriting. She would multiply the recipes many times over for iftar[5] dinners or masjid events. She did work magic in that kitchen, but the magic was in her ability to follow the steps, add the correct amounts, and maintain patience with the results.

By my mother's side I learned about the importance of rules and order in the kitchen. She would play Qur'an or Islamic lectures as she carefully chopped and prepared vegetables. When we were older, my mother assigned this task to myself and Sadiya, my sister. She would lecture us on cleanliness, washing our hands before we began, wiping down the countertops

---

[5] Meal to break the fast, usually during the month of Ramadan.

and washing the cutting boards in scalding hot water. "You can't put in halfhearted efforts, and expect perfect results. The Prophet Muhammad - peace be upon him - said the one who works is a friend of Allah, and the one who does not work is his outright enemy," she would say many times. My mother did work in that hot and cramped kitchen. I wondered many times if Jummah[6] prayers would be as packed if it weren't for the lunches that my mother prepared in that small kitchen.

Sadiya would often earn my mother's anger and frustration by not following the exact recipes. She would chop the onions into chunks, instead of small cubes, or refuse to use the measuring cups and spoons, opting instead to pour flour and baking soda directly into the mixing bowl. At one particular dinner, my sister did not allow the roll dough to rise. This resulted in hard flat disks that she actually tried to serve. I still remember my sister defiantly taking a bite out of one of those rolls and flippantly saying, "It tastes just fine to me," as she stubbornly chewed and tried to swallow it, nearly gagging.

Eventually, my mother banned Sadiya from the kitchen. I wanted my mother to be pleased with me, so I would follow her directions step-by-step, and marvel at the results. Her recipes were tested and always came

---

[6] Jummah is the term for Friday congregational prayers.

out perfectly. In truth, I hated the process. My back would hurt as I stood at the cutting board. The heat of the oven and stove made me sweaty. I disliked my hands smelling like onions and how long it took to wash biscuit dough off of them, but I liked the results. I found security in the fact that, if I followed the recipe, things would turn out properly. My mother and I would work around each other. I would roll out the dough, cut them into round disks, and put them in the oven so that they would be done before the pies needed to be go in. My mother would place the fish in the fryer, and I would remove the golden-brown fillets, using brown paper bags to drain the excess oil. We didn't talk much. The kitchen was filled with the noise of Qur'an playing on my mother's CD player. It was a familiar routine, and one that we repeated countless times, preparing for countless lunches, dinners, and iftar events.

Just as I learned about the importance of following my mother's recipes in the Masjid kitchen, I learned about following the Qur'an and Sunnah[7] upstairs in the masjid's prayer area. My father, Dawood Abdul-Aziz, was known as Imam[8] Dawood in the community. Rarely did a Friday pass when my father didn't offer the Jummah Khutbah[9]. There, I learned life

---

[7] Sunnah is the term for the words and deeds practiced by the Prophet Muhammad.

[8] Leader of an Islamic community.

[9] Khutbah is the Islamic term for sermon.

lessons based on stories from the holy Qur'an and reflections on the Prophet Muhammad's life. My father wove stories of the Prophet into reflections on the modern-day trials that the community faced. He artfully added a few jokes here and there in order to keep the congregation's attention.

One story he often came back to was that of Prophet Yusuf, whose life was filled with trial after trial, from being left in a well to die by his own brothers, to being sold as a slave by traders, to being jailed for a crime he did not commit. "Yet throughout all of this, years of enslavement, imprisonment, and separation from his family, Prophet Yusuf, never forgot his duty to worship Allah, and spread the message of Islam. When his brothers came to him, he didn't seek revenge. Instead, he gave them the grain that they needed, and in the end, his patience was rewarded and his dream was fulfilled. As the Holy Qur'an states, 'Is the reward for good anything but good?' We have to keep this example in mind when we deal with petty arguments. Prophet Yusuf fed his brothers even though they had betrayed him. It wasn't a small argument about clothes. When faced with the trials of life, we should seek to exhibit as much patience as Prophet Yusuf." My father's comment about trivial arguments was a direct hit at a few of the brothers who had stopped speaking to each other due to a disagreement over a Saint's jersey.

9

It was these two models that formed the foundation of my psyche. If I followed my mother's recipes, and the examples from the Qur'an and sunnah that my father extolled, then how could things go wrong? Certainly, with patience, faith in God, and the examples provided by my parents, things would always turn out well for me.

Yet, as I became an adult, life taught me lessons that could only be learned through experience. It became clear that life wasn't always so black and white, and as much as I sought to follow the correct recipe, there was a possibility that the end result could still turn out poorly.

Chapter 1

It has always seemed interesting to me the way in which unfortunate events unfold. In books and movies, there is a small omen or foreshadowing to give the viewer a hint that something is going to happen that will throw the protagonist's life off course. Yet is it the same in real life? Is there always a sign, a hint, or an inkling that things aren't going to continue as planned? Looking back at my life, I think sometimes there are. It's usually a small hint that at the moment may seem insignificant, yet looking back that sign signified something was about to change forever.

Like the storm that swept through New Orleans, when I was a teenager. There had been many smaller storms leading up to the big one, Katrina. Nature had offered warnings; the waters were hotter than they had been in years and it had snowed the winter before the storm hit. All these were signs that the next storm that made landfall would be huge. Maybe many didn't realize how big it would end up being, but no one could say that there weren't signs. As I sat that day on the bathroom floor, my mind was on the small signs, as well as the bigger ones that I had chosen to ignore in my own life.

I sat on the bed, our bed, the cheerful floral comforter provided little comfort for me. The sweet photos that had adorned the wall just the day before, were now strewn on the floor. I myself had snatched them from the wall and thrown them down. I had slammed them down hard enough to make noise, but not with enough force to break the glass nor the picture frames. Frustratingly, the plush carpeting we had so carefully chosen months before had softened their fall. The sickening taste of bile sat in the back of my throat. Soon, the tears began to fall again. Despite my best efforts, and in spite of my desire to be resolved to Allah's plan, the same word repeatedly escaped from my lips. "Why, why, why?" I questioned. To whom, I didn't know. I tried to take some deep breaths, and calm myself down. Yet I began to hyperventilate and soon I was retching.

I ran to the bathroom and threw up again. This would be the fourth time today. The bit of tea that I had consumed had left my stomach long ago. Now I

12

threw up a foul yellow substance—stomach acid that burned my throat and brought tears to my eyes. I lay down on the cool tile of the bathroom floor. I attempted to catch my breath but failed.

Despite the fact that I hadn't eaten a full meal in days, and what I had eaten was promptly rejected from my body, the baby still managed to kick and stretch inside of me. This was supposed to be a time of intense joy and happy anticipation, instead I felt nothing but pain, hurt and bubbling deep inside. Anger. The life that I had once known, the one I had so carefully worked for was crumbling down around me. I wanted to stop this downward spiral...this unraveling of my life, yet I felt just as helpless as the baby inside of me. Indeed, the "why?" that continually crept from my lips was as nonsensical as a baby's babbles.

I wasn't sure if I was asking "Why me?" or "Why now?" or "Why her?" I only knew that I was overcome with the unfairness of it all. I was amazed by how easily one's life could fall apart like the beads falling off of a broken necklace one-by-one. This wasn't the first time I had felt the intensity of suffering. Yet in that moment, the pain of this situation seemed too much to bear. I rinsed my mouth with cool water and washed my face. I stared into my brown eyes in the bathroom mirror. There were deep bags under my eyes and my skin looked more pale than usual. My skin had taken on an almost yellow tone that reminded me of the bile I had just thrown up. I wanted to call my mother or my best friend Zayna. However, I didn't want them to see me this way, and I was ashamed of how far I had allowed all of this to go.

Instead, I returned to the bedroom and looked down at the framed photos that I had yanked from the wall. In one, I wore my wedding dress. I looked down demurely at my bouquet of lavender roses. My husband smiled widely, proudly at the camera. The photo captured a moment that now seemed alien to me. The girl in the photo knew nothing of this pain. I yearned to be that girl once again. Our names, "Anaya & Jahid," were embossed on the bottom in delicate cursive, along with our wedding date. I remembered placing that photo into the thick gold frame and proudly hanging it on the wall of our new home. Then, our future had seemed so full of hope. I had questioned whether or not I was worthy of such happiness.

How had things changed so drastically? When did things start to fall apart? If I was honest with myself, I could admit that there had been hints and signs leading up to this day. I had chosen to ignore them all. I wanted to believe that this man, this house, and this life were my happy ending. This was supposed to be my reward for doing things the *right* way. I laid on the bed, in much the same position as the baby inside of me and began to examine every choice that lead me to that point.

I was a college student when I got married. I had known my fiancé for less than six months. I often wondered, *why did I marry him?* The truth was, I thought he was the answer to all of my prayers.

A few weeks before Jahid had called my father, expressing his interest in marrying me, I had prayed for Allah's help.

Chapter 2

I was homeschooled as a child. While I did take field trips and have play dates with other homeschooled children, my days were mostly focused around books, my mother's explanations of my lessons, and spending time in the masjid. I knew that my parents wanted to protect me and I was grateful for their protection. As I got older, I would complete lessons on my laptop. I received emails from an advisory teacher who critiqued my essays and corrected my math assignments. It was lonely at times, yet since I was to go at my own pace, I was able to finish my high school coursework in just three years.

At seventeen years old, I began the process of enrolling in college. I could see the worry in my mother's eyes. She tried to encourage me to enroll in a smaller community college instead of the larger four-year school. "Don't you think that would be easier? You could finish two years at the junior college and then transfer to the university," she said. In my heart I knew that once I had a two-year degree, I would again have to go through the process of going back to school. I wanted the four-year school. I wanted the big buildings, the school clubs and meetings, the promise of expansion. It excited me and I wanted to be a part of it all. I was a baby bird ready to depart the nest.

Yet, I knew my parents were afraid for me. They prayed that I wouldn't be tricked by Shaytan[10]. My parents often mentioned that Shaytan lurked just around every corner. Truly, Shaytan became the boogeyman, ready to do harm to unsuspecting children who didn't follow their parents' rules and adults who didn't follow the Qur'an and Sunnah. Leading up to me beginning school they gave me warnings and lectures about things I should be sure to do and avoid doing.

It wasn't that I didn't understand and agree with my parents' warnings. I had attended Islamic classes at the masjid from a young age. There I memorized Qur'an and stories from Hadith[11] under Sister Qadira's watchful eye. Sister Qadira, who led the girls' class for as long as I could remember, became like a second mother to me over the years. Her long flowing skirts and tunics became as familiar to me as the thick green and gold prayer rugs of the masjid itself. Her friendly smile and sweet voice could turn sharp and reprimanding to the girls who chose to spend the class time gossiping and chatting instead of focusing on their recitation. Her lessons often included examples that echoed those of my parents: guard your modesty, keep

---

[10] The devil.
[11] Hadith are books of the words and events of the Prophet Muhammad's life.

17

up your prayers, fast, give to charity, don't associate others with Allah—those were the rules we should follow if we wanted the rewards of this world and the hereafter. I saw firsthand what happened to those chatty girls who didn't follow them. A few of the girls talked to boys in secret, dropped out of Sister Qadira's classes, or stopped wearing hijab[12]. I would still see some of them around the city occasionally. Those who didn't come to the masjid anymore, often wore a look of guilt when they would see me with my father.

My parents were converts to Islam. They both left the Christian tradition of their parents and chose Islam as a way of life. My father changed his name from David to Dawood. The former being the biblical form of the name, the latter the Arabic variation. My mother went from Mildred to Malikah. She always said that it was an easy change because she had hated the name Mildred. The clothes that we wore, foods that we ate and belief system that we followed were much different from many others around us. The city of New Orleans had few Muslims. I remember from a young age, wearing a traditional head scarf, being very aware that we didn't eat pork or grocery store meat, and we were seldom allowed to visit neighborhood friends in case they tried to feed us

---

[12] Islamic head covering worn by women.

something haram or expose us to some forbidden movie or video game.

I took my parents words to heart. My sister, Sadiya, sometimes did what she wanted behind my parents' backs and lied about it or found ways to cover up her misbehavior. Yet, I wanted none of that. When I started college, I came home promptly after classes, and if I was going to be late, I would call and let my parents know. I didn't hang out in the student lounge where students laughed, joked, and openly flirted with each other. I went straight to class, brought my lunch from home and ate on the picnic tables in the quad. I would then go to my student job, first tutoring remedial students in English and later in the library stacking books in the long rows.

It may have seemed like a boring life to some, but it suited me. I enjoyed my classes and the in-depth discussions. It was my first time being in an environment with so many different races, nationalities, viewpoints, and religions. I remember debating on Plato's and Aristotle's view of God in my philosophy class. There were students that were Christian, Buddhist, Atheist, Hindu, and then me. Many times, I would simply observe the interactions and debates. I was too shy to raise my hand and offer my opinion. Even so, I could physically feel my brain expanding in my skull. It was exhilarating.

My one sore spot was French. I couldn't get the pronunciation down, and the verb forms confused me. I was a perfectionist, and the C's that my teacher gave me struck me to my core. One day I visited the language lab asking for help.

"We have a student-to-student tutoring program," the smiling woman at the desk stated. "We have a great French tutor. He's so very helpful." She scribbled down the contact information for someone named Colson. *He?* I thought to myself.

"Ok...are there any female French tutors?" I asked. Hoping that there was.

"Not at this time," she replied. "I can put you on the waiting list until one becomes available," she finished. She looked at me, ready to grab back the slip of paper on which she had written the contact info. Yet I didn't give it back to her. Midterms were coming up, and so I accepted Colson as a tutor.

I told my mother I would be receiving French tutoring on Tuesdays and Thursdays, and would be coming home late. I omitted the fact that my tutor was male. I knew my parents would sooner have me drop the course or even fail rather than sit alone with a male tutor. I felt a little guilty about not telling my mother the complete truth, but I reasoned it wasn't as bad as what Sadiya was doing and I didn't have any ill intentions. I only wanted to raise my French grade. No harm in that.

During our first session, we met at the library in one of the study carrels. He parked his skateboard outside the door against the wall. He wore a Bob Marley T-Shirt and Converse sneakers. We went over my vocabulary words for the week and he corrected my pronunciation. He then complimented my hijab. It was navy blue with a pattern of small purple flowers.

"Nice scarf," he had said. "Why do you wear that?" I sighed, I had been asked this question many times before. I was one of only four or five covered Muslim girls on our campus. "I'm Muslim," I stated, turning the page in my textbook to my homework assignment. He looked at me expectantly, as if I should say something more. "I see you're Muslim, but *why do you wear that?*" his honey colored eyes seemed to bore through me. I wasn't expecting a philosophical discussion now. "In Islam, a woman should guard her modesty, and we're only allowed to show our hair and other parts of our body to our fathers, brothers and uncles," I replied. It was the religious definition that had been presented to me many times, yet why did it sound hollow to my ears? I began to sweat.

Sensing my discomfort, he said, "It's ok, you don't have to say anymore." His voice was so softly accented. If I didn't know he was French, I might miss it altogether. He glanced at the open page of my textbook. "Is this your homework?" he asked. We spent the rest of the hour going over verb formations and vocabulary drills not bringing up the scarf subject again.

Later that day, as I stacked books in the library, an intense anger came over me. *Why had I allowed him to question me like that?* I thought of all the ways I could have responded. I could have said, "It's not any of your concern" or "I came to you for tutoring not for you to question the way I dress." Yet, I had to admit, the question hit a sore spot in my mind. I knew the textbook answer and the verse of Qur'an that commanded me to do it, but there had to be a deeper reason. What angered me was the more I searched my heart for a deeper reason, the more it became clear that I just didn't have one.

Colson's question hit deeply, yet I couldn't pinpoint why. I knew that wearing hijab was my choice, yet I also knew that in order to remain in my parents' home, I must honor their rules. Since I was a young girl, covering my hair, dressing modestly, and not having any male friends were just a few of the rules. On the college campus students dressed any and every way. Some of the young girls had dreadlocks or dyed their hair outlandish colors. One girl in my math class had shaved her head bald. And there I was in my hijab. It was just a piece of fabric, but in a way, it put a barrier between myself and the other students. I appreciated that barrier at times. Yet, I also had to admit that at other times the barrier worked against me.

However, I never took off my hijab. The thought of exposing my long braids made me feel naked. The hijab was one tenet of my faith I never thought of breaking. But Colson's question still made me feel uneasy. My sister had always been the one to test my parents' rules. If she didn't like one of their rules, she simply wouldn't follow it. She was often punished for her misbehavior. Her defiance seemed silly to me. She knew she would eventually be caught and punished, but that wasn't enough to deter her from disobeying my parents. And maybe it wasn't true that I had a deeper faith than my sister. Maybe I was just more afraid of the punishment, or more interested in staying in my parents' good graces than my sister.

It was in college that I truly began to face the reality of my choices. Colson's question especially hit me because the hijab had begun to weigh greatly upon me. Growing up, I came to an awareness that my hijab carried a great weight within and around it. Yet that year, at times, the load almost became a burden.

I was a young girl when I first learned that my clothing was a means of distance between myself and others around me. I was playing Barbies at a next-door neighbor's house. My playmate paused to ask, "Why do you wear that thing on your head?" At a loss for words, I didn't answer. Her father, however, jumped in and said, "She's probably wearing it so the rain won't get on her hair." It *was* raining that afternoon, and I remember watching the drops hit the window. We both shrugged and continued playing. I didn't possess the vocabulary to answer such a question.

One day at the college, I raised my hand to answer a question in biology lab. The instructor said, "You with the thing on your head," as she gestured towards me. She could have said, "You in the pink shirt" or "You near the window" but no, she chose to reference my headscarf.

In a literature class, the professor was trying to explain the word *"manteau"* to another student. He said, "It's like if she took that thing on her head and wrapped it around her," he joked. I didn't laugh. My cheeks burned.

That wasn't the only time my scarf became a joke. While I worked as a tutor that same year, one of the other student workers put a t-shirt on his head and said, "Look, I'm Anaya." Rather than confront the situation, I asked to be placed in a different position on campus. I left my job tutoring English and got a placement in the library. I looked at the many carts of books ready to be stacked in the long seemingly endless aisles and thought to myself: *This suits me better, anyway.*

So, I guess Colson's question came at just the right time. I began to question if it would be easier to just remove it. I didn't like feeling like an outsider. There were a few girls on campus who were Muslim but didn't cover. They went to the masjid in Kenner, and when I tried befriending them, they gave me cold *salams*[13], and continued their conversations in fluent Arabic. They seemed to easily blend in with the crowd on campus. In a way, I envied how they floated anonymously through campus. They didn't wear their religion outwardly as I did. I knew that if I was going to keep wearing hijab, that it had to come from a greater place than because my parents said so. One day, unexpectedly, I found that greater justification, when I was least expecting it.

---

[13] Greetings of peace.

Chapter 3

It was a spring day, and I was just leaving my library job. I didn't have my license during my first year in school. Each afternoon I would wait for my father to text me, letting me know that he was on his way. However, that afternoon, my father had let me know that he wouldn't be able to pick me up. There was a meeting in the masjid which he had to attend. I would have to take the bus. I had taken the bus home a few times and it was an easy trip. I would catch the Elysian Fields bus, which stopped right on campus. It would take me a few miles down, and then it was a short walk from the stop to the house.

Yet that day, as I approached the bus stop, taking out my transit card, the sky seemed to open up. Buckets of rain began to pour down upon me and I was soaking wet within a few minutes. This wasn't unusual for a New Orleans spring or summer day. It wasn't uncommon for unexpected storms to hit fast and hard. I was usually able to sit out the rain in one of the campus buildings while I waited for one of my parents or Sadiya to come get me, but this shower had me soaked before I could even walk back to the nearest building. My socks and sneakers were soggy within minutes, and I worried about my textbooks as the water soaked my backpack.

Suddenly, a car pulled up to me. The window of the burgundy Toyota opened and a voice from inside yelled: *"Assalam Alaikum[14]! Assalam Alaikum!"* I didn't recognize the car, but I walked up to the window to see who it was. I could barely hear her above the storm that was quickly becoming more intense. "Hi, I'm Zayna," the girl yelled. "I see you sometimes at the bus stop. I was wondering do you need a ride? They say it's going to be a flash flood."

The young girl driving looked to be about nineteen or twenty years old. A thin royal blue scarf was wrapped loosely around her head, yet I could still see thick black hair peeking out from beneath the thin fabric of her scarf. She had big dark brown almost black eyes and a friendly smile. I hesitated, but a nearly deafening thunderclap echoed from the sky, causing

---

[14] Peace be unto you.

both of us to jump. The water was rising fast, and was already nearly up to my ankles.

I remembered my parents' warnings about smiling faces sometimes masking evil intentions. I considered my choices at the moment. I could continue to wait for the bus in the pouring rain or I could walk back to campus and call one of my parents to come get me. Neither of those choices felt right when there was a friendly face and a dry car ready to give me a ride. I decided to trust her and I jumped into the car. "I'm so sorry," I said as we began to drive off, "your seat is going to get all wet." My tunic and jeans were drenched and now so was her seat.

"It's ok. Don't worry about it. Listen, this rain isn't going to stop and it won't be safe to drive soon. Can we go to my place for a little while?" She didn't wait for me to answer. In just a few minutes we were pulling into the parking lot of an apartment building close to the college. We ran from the car as the rain poured down upon us.

We laughed at ourselves nearly slipping on the linoleum of her front entrance. "This is crazy," Zayna said as she removed her sandals. I began to take off my sneakers and wondered if I should sit. Water was already beginning to pool at my feet on her floor. She ran to a back room and returned without her scarf on, offering me thick fluffy towels. I thanked her and wrapped one of the towels around myself, using it to absorb some of the water from my clothing. Her apartment had a only a few furnishings. There was a beige futon on one wall and a black armchair on another. On the kitchen counter was a small TV and her laptop computer. A few textbooks were on a round coffee table. In the corner was a prayer rug neatly folded and a bookshelf held a Qur'an and a few other religious books. The place smelled like sandalwood and despite the sparse furnishings it was inviting.

I wrapped the thick towel around myself and sat on the futon. Zayna was already in the small kitchen pouring water into a tea kettle and grabbing some mismatched mugs from the cabinet. "You know, I always see you on campus and sometimes at the bus stop, but I never had the chance to speak to you." There were only a few girls in hijab on campus and most of them were foreign students who came to the USA to earn master's degrees or Ph.D.'s. I had never seen this girl on campus. "I see you in your hijab," she continued, "and I think how strong you must be to wear it every day. I really admire your faith, masha Allah." I was confused, then I realized that I had seen her before. Without her scarf on I realized that I had seen her in the library many times. I had never seen her in hijab, and I wondered what made her decide to wear it today.

"I'm just talking and talking and didn't even get your name," Zayna stated.

"Anaya," I said. "I think I have seen you around campus, in the library. I work there most mornings," I continued.

She looked down as if a little embarrassed. "I don't usually wear hijab," she said, as if reading my mind. "I have even been thinking about if it is even really required of us. Yet, I was listening to a lecture the other day and one of the things the sister said about the many benefits of hijab is that it allows us as Muslims to recognize one another ...It's crazy how I was wearing it today and I was able to help you, and maybe the hijab was part of the reason that you allowed me to." I mulled this over. Truthfully, I probably wouldn't have accepted Zayna's ride that day if she wasn't in hijab. I also thought about the fact that she likely wouldn't have offered me the ride if she hadn't seen me around campus in my scarf. The hijab protected me on that day, and I thought about what else the hijab was protecting me from, perhaps things I had never even considered.

The storm that day was one of the biggest floods outside of a hurricane that New Orleans had seen in years. I ended up staying in Zayna's small apartment for hours talking with her. She told me that her parents were from India. Her mother had died when she was a young girl. A few years prior to her starting college, her father had remarried a woman in her twenties. She now had half-sisters who were in prek and kindergarten. Besides her father, step-mother, and half-sisters, Zayna had few family members in the states except for some distant cousins, and so it was easy for her to uproot herself from Northern Louisiana and come to New Orleans. I imagined she felt it was a fresh start.

It was late at night when the roads had cleared enough for my parents to come get me. As I hopped into the car, my parents looked at Zayna's apartment suspiciously. "Who's this friend of yours?" my father asked first.

I dared not tell him we had only just met today. "Her name's Zayna. I see her at the library sometimes. She's studying nursing," I said. Zayna had come outside to walk me to the car. As we pulled off, I could see her opening the door of her apartment.

"Who does she live with?" It was my mother's turn now. She glared at the door to Zayna's apartment as if she was looking for answers.

"She lives alone," I replied. "Her family is in Lafayette." I knew my parents now sat in silent judgement of her. The fact that she didn't cover and that she was a young woman who lived alone were both facts that provided more than enough reason to do so. I sat back in my seat awaiting their comments. Yet they said nothing. I closed my eyes and took a deep, grateful breath.

31

I thought of Zayna that day as I sat on the bed in tears. I imagined what she would say if I ever got the courage to tell her about all that was happening. Zayna was a fighter. She was someone whom I looked up to and would always fiercely defend, and she had proven to be the same for me over the years. Yet, I still didn't have the strength to call upon her. The thought of explaining it all...putting everything I had been going through into words, made me want to vomit again. Instead of calling her, I pulled the floral comforter up to my ears and continued to contemplate all the choices that led me there.

Chapter 4

The next time I had a scheduled tutoring session with Colson, I went over in my mind how I would bring up the subject of hijab and what I would say. I had let myself down on two fronts during my interaction with him. I felt I had missed out on an opportunity to do *dawah*, to share my religion with him. I had the chance to open his eyes to the beauty of Islam and had failed. I had also allowed his limited understanding of Islam to make me question my religion. In my mind that was the ultimate defeat.

During our weekly Islamic studies classes I had always been taught by my parents and Sister Qadira the importance of having an unwavering faith in Islam. Many times, I heard my father say, "Those who even have an atom's weight worth of pride will not enter *Jannah*. Do you know what pride is?" he would ask. "Pride is doubt in the religion," he would answer his own question.

I remember sitting in Islamic studies classes with Sister Qadira and under her watchful eye going over all of the verses of the Qur'an that began, "Oh you who believe."

33

"*Ya Ayyuhalatheena amanoo*," she would recite slowly. "These are all warnings for those who believe in Allah, those who have faith." One particular verse she spent a long time on, she translated as, "O ye who believe! Enter into Islam whole-heartedly; and follow not the footsteps of the evil one; for he is to you an avowed enemy." Of course, "the evil one" was Shaytan ready to whisper in the ears of the believers and cause us to be diverted from the straight path.

"When the Qur'an says, 'wholeheartedly,' that means you can't take what parts you want and leave others. This isn't a buffet religion. You have to accept it all and be amongst the believers or risk misery in this *dunya* and a severe punishment in the hereafter," Sister Qadira had sternly warned. Her ebony colored eyes seemed to look through us and directly into our hearts, attempting to determine which of us doubted the truth in her words.

On that afternoon with Colson, I wanted to bring up the subject and explain the wisdom of *hijab* to him in a way that he could understand. My mind was on this challenge as I sat in the study room waiting to be tutored. Yet, when he arrived I felt strangely flustered.

"Salut," he said nonchalantly. He sat in the study carrel and pulled my textbook closer to him. He had on shorts, flip flops and another Bob Marley shirt.

This one had the singer with his locs framing his face similar to a lion's mane.

"Hi," was all I could squeak out.

"If you want to learn French, we have to get you speaking in French," he said. "You want to start thinking in the language...it will become more natural for you if you use the new words you're learning all the time."

"Are you from France?" I asked.

"My father is French. My mother is from New York, though," he paused looking at me intently. "She's black, and my father is white. Is that what you were wondering?" he questioned. I shrugged. He always threw me off with his questions. I doubted I would ever be used to his bluntness and the way his eyes examined mine.

Truthfully, I was wondering about his heritage. His skin was fair, a shade similar to coco-butter. His hair was a curly afro that coupled with his amber eyes made him look not completely white or black. Now that I knew he was bi-racial, it made sense, but I felt like I should have never asked.

"No," I said. "I was just wondering how you became fluent."

Now it was his turn to shrug. "I spend every summer there visiting my father's family," he said. We continued the lesson, again with more vocabulary words and some verb formations. The session was almost ending, when I remembered how I had wanted to talk about *hijab* with him.

"The other day, you asked me why I cover my hair," I began. He looked at me confusedly. "Well, I know you may not ever understand, but the *hijab* has been a protection for me in many ways." At this he raised his eyebrow.

"You know, you don't have to convince me," he said. "If you feel comfortable in it and it makes you happy, that's good," he finished. He seemed ready to finish the session and leave.

"It's not about making me happy. There are some things that you dislike that are good for you and some things you may like that are bad for you...Some days I feel great in it and sometimes I might want to blend in, but I know in my heart it's a protection for me," I explained. Suddenly, I felt silly for even trying to explain all this to him. Why did his opinion matter to me so much anyway? I started packing my messenger bag to leave. Looking up, I was surprised to see him still staring at me intently.

"You are very strong to wear it even though it must be hard for you sometimes. I shouldn't have brought it up," he said. "*Salut,*" he finished with a nod as he exited the room.

Strong.

36

He has used the same word to describe me as Zayna had only a few days prior. I wondered how two people who barely knew me could use the exact same word to describe me. It wasn't a word I would have chosen to describe myself. How did they both see something in me that I doubted existed in myself. In a way, I felt like a fraud. I shrugged off those feelings and left for work.

I remember later that afternoon, as I shelved books in the library, thinking about the exchange with Colson and also the one with Zayna. I just wanted to please Allah, and follow the Qur'an as best I could. I really didn't think that there was anything special about me. I honestly didn't feel any stronger than anyone else.

I thought of my sister, who moved away from home at eighteen years old. She only covered her hair when she came around the family, out of respect for my parents. She lived a life that was so different from mine, that it was hard to connect with Sadiya besides the perfunctory small talk that we exchanged when she would stop by the house. As I started college, she was in school trying to get a CNA certificate. She had gone through many roommates in the five years since she left home. It seemed like every time we spoke she was living in a different area of the city. Her car was always breaking down, and she would be forced to meekly ask my parents for money to repair it.

Although, I didn't always like my parents' rules, I understood that they were meant as a protection for me. The thought of stepping into the unknown, like Sadiya did, made my heart race. Even though I didn't agree with all of the choices that my sister made, I felt that it took a certain amount of bravery to leave everything she knew, and face the unknown the way that she did.

Sadiya wasn't the only one. When I was entering middle school, there were nearly twenty of us girls in Sister Qadira's weekend class. As the years wore on, the numbers thinned and thinned. It was hard for us navigating being Muslim and African-American. Outside of the safe spaces of our homes and within the masjid, we felt too foreign for the neighborhood kids and our classmates for those of us in public schools. And when we visited other mosques, we were often ignored or shunned. We weren't Arab, Indian or Pakistani, and in their spaces, it was sometimes hard to find a smiling or welcoming face. I knew that most of the girls wanted to experience life outside of our tight knit community. Many of them tested the waters, and unfortunately, some got dragged into the undertow.

I remained in the safety of my parents' home. I would spend hours on weekends reading and studying in my bedroom. I found peace in the comfort of the masjid. The thick wool rugs, the scent of incense and the sound of Qur'an CDs softly playing surrounded me like a favorite blanket. The thought of stepping outside of those spaces filled me with anxiety. It did take some fortitude for me to begin college, but I knew in my heart that I wanted a degree. I wanted to be a teacher and going to college was the only way I would be able to fulfill that dream. So, every day I would put my fears aside and attend my classes.

In my classes, I would rarely raise my hand. Although I sat near the front of the classrooms and auditoriums, I didn't answer or ask questions. I chose instead to absorb all that was being said, while taking notes, and reading along in my textbooks. Sometimes I didn't understand my professor's explanations. Being homeschooled, I had become used to reading and processing information alone. Now I had six different instructors, each with different teaching styles. So, I created a cocoon for myself in classes. Listening while reading my textbook at the same time helped me process the information in my own way. And it had worked for me, until my French professor expected me to verbalize what he had just taught. I started reading the lessons ahead of time to be prepared for the conversation portion of class, but sometimes he would throw in words and phrases that were not in the lesson.

During our last session, Colson had insisted that I speak in French. I knew it was good, still, it made me uncomfortable. My shyness was a barrier that I had to overcome if I was going to be successful in college, but I didn't want to cross too many boundaries and become like those my parents had warned me against.

"Some people become so interested in their worldly life, that they forget about the hereafter," my mother said. "Don't be like those people. In the end, they will be the losers."

That day, when I had returned home on the bus, I found my sister sitting with my father at the kitchen table. I was surprised to see her. It felt as if thinking about her had willed her to visit. She wore a gold colored turban and hoop earrings. "I'll let you use the Honda for the weekend, Sadiya, but I really want you to ask yourself, why are you having all these problems? Sometimes Allah tests a person in order to bring them closer to Him. Maybe you can decide when the test is over. You know, Allah says that if we come to him walking, he will come to us running."

As my father spoke, Sadiya sat silently. She nodded gently, but her deep brown eyes were downcast. She was running her fingers along the floral embroidery on the placemat, as she listened to words that must've sounded very familiar to her by now. My parents had a Honda Civic that my mother mostly drove. It was clear that Sadiya was asking to borrow it. I assumed her raggedy car had broken down, again.

Looking up as I entered the kitchen, Sadiya looked relieved to see me. "*Assalam Alaikum*, little sis! How's school?"

I gave her the usual response. My father nodded at me, as he left the room. He returned with the keys to the car. Sadiya thanked him and offered an awkward hug as she left.

"Your sister stays getting into some mess," my father began. "Her car broke down *again*, and if she doesn't get to work on time this weekend she'll be fired." He shook his head profusely. "I swear, *Shaytan* can come whisper in your ear and make the dunya seem attractive. But who do you have to fall back on when you're out in the world with no one to turn to?" It was a rhetorical question. I had now taken Sadiya's place as a listener. I simply nodded as he continued on.

"Where's Momma," I finally interrupted, hoping my question might change the topic. I had heard this lecture many times. I had studying to do and a paper to write.

"She's at the store. Should be back soon," my father said and took a deep sigh. I looked at his face. I could see the disappointment in his eyes. I guessed he was reflecting on Sadiya. My father always told us that he had found Islam after "experimenting in the *dunya*" as he called it. He never got too much into detail, but it was clear that he had taken part in a few petty crimes and spent time in jail. I had seen an old photo of my father wearing jeans, a few gold chains, and an earring. I knew that my father only wanted to protect us from the path that he had gone down, but it did seem a little deluded for him to think that Sadiya wouldn't make mistakes and bad choices the same way he himself had. I didn't get into it though. I had also heard him say many times, "A smart person learns from his own mistakes, a wise person learns from the mistakes of others, and a fool will just never learn."

Chapter 5

Looking back, I am shocked at how singularly focused I was during that time. I would take fifteen to eighteen credits each semester in school, going directly from classes and labs to my job at the library. In the evenings, I would go directly home or to the computer lab to study. Once I introduced Zayna to my parents, and they learned of her past, they began to trust her, and sometimes I would be allowed to visit her apartment after school. Together we would study, or sometimes just talk. She was just as determined as I was to earn good grades and finish school. I divided my weekends between studying and completing assignments at home or attending classes and functions at the masjid.

Now I wonder why I didn't allow myself to have some fun in those days. Yes, Zayna and I spent many afternoons chatting and laughing but I didn't allow myself to fully experience college life. I didn't go to basketball games or get involved in any clubs. The cocoon that I put around myself acted as a wall to keep out anything that stood in the way of me succeeding. However, a cocoon isn't a permanent resting place. Eventually you have to emerge from it changed.

On Monday and Wednesday mornings I attended an African-American literature class, which I loved. There, I was introduced to authors I had never heard of before, and the writings often touched on historical events, which lead to heated discussions. Although I rarely raised my hand, I enjoyed listening to all the different points of view. The professor, Dr. Bryan, was one of the few African-American instructors on campus and his class became a safe space for many black students in the mostly white school.

In one class Dr. Bryan had us read essays and poems related to the murder of Emmett Till. The discussion that day in class was on America's disregard for the loss of black lives from the time of slavery all the way to Hurricane Katrina. I was deep in thought about this after class was over, so much so that I almost didn't see Colson waiting for me outside of my classroom.

"Hi," he said. He wore jeans and a t-shirt. This one featured a silhouette of Nina Simone.

"Oh, hi," I replied. I was surprised to see him outside of our tutoring sessions. He stood leaning against the wall. His messenger bag was on the floor next to him. He appeared to be waiting for someone. I began to walk away towards the quad when he picked up his bag and began to follow along.

"How was your class?" he asked. He had fallen into step with me and didn't seem like he was going to explain his appearance anytime soon.

"It was interesting," I replied. He didn't say anything further. I was headed towards the picnic benches under the rows of towering Oak trees at the center of campus. This was my usual lunch spot. I liked sitting outside and reading or people watching as I ate. The shade from the trees, as well as the moss hanging from them provided a sense of solitude for me. We were silent as we walked.

"Have you taken any courses with Dr. Bryan?" I asked in an attempt to fill the silence.

"I had him for a writing class my first semester, but I dropped it," he said casually. We had reached my usual spot. I took off my backpack and sat down. I looked at him incredulously. The thought of anyone dropping a class with Dr. Bryan was beyond me. Colson sat across from me at the table, placing his messenger bag beside him.

"Why? He's a great instructor." My mind was still filled with the thoughts and ideas that had been expressed during today's class.

"I couldn't take all that talk about race...I mean, I feel like that kind of rhetoric just keeps us

45

stuck." I tried to keep myself from rolling my eyes. I took a few deep breaths.

"What do you mean?" I asked. I wanted to give him a chance to explain himself. Dr. Bryan's class was one of the few places where people of color with many different points of view felt free to express themselves and feel heard instead of silenced.

"I mean, African-Americans in this country focus on the past too much. How can you ever move forward if you continue to constantly dredge up yesterday's pain?"

"Yesterday's pain? The pain we feel is not only about events that happened yesterday," I could feel myself getting angry. "Members of my family lost their homes and everything else in the storm, and now our insurance is so high we can barely make the payments. Parts of the city are still destroyed, years later."

"Anaya, I came to New Orleans as a volunteer in my school just after the storm. Katrina is the only reason I decided to come to school here, against my parents' wishes. I'm sorry about what happened to your family, but you can't blame that on race."

I looked at Colson carefully. I didn't know that he had been a volunteer. Yet, it didn't seem like his experience offered him a full view of race relations in my city.

46

"Do you know that someone in the 9th ward got less to rebuild their home then someone in an affluent area? Yet, it will cost the same to rebuild the home in the 9th ward and the home in the Lakefront. What about those who only got a fraction of what it would cost to rebuild their homes, only because they live in a Black area? And to make matters worse, those same families who are not getting enough to rebuild, have been paying nearly twice the insurance rates for years, and they still do."

This was the most I had ever said to Colson, and he seemed somewhat taken aback by me. I tried to calm down, but I couldn't. All my thoughts and feelings about the situation in my city started to come out. It was like I couldn't bottle them up anymore. In many of my classes, the students were from Kenner, Metairie or the West Bank. These were suburbs that weren't greatly affected by the storm. Then there were students like Colson, who came to New Orleans from other states. Some felt like they were giving something back or doing the city a favor by coming, yet they didn't know what it was really like to struggle through what we had, and they had comfort in the fact that after a few years they would return to their home states.

"I have heard about situations like that," Colson said. "But is that about race or money? When I was out in the Bayou, I saw white families in the same predicament. I understand it's a sad situation, but you can't blame everything on race."

47

"After Katrina, they left the bodies of black people sitting out for weeks. They cleaned up the white areas first," I said. "I remember seeing some on the news. They didn't even have enough respect to cover those bodies." Instead of feeling angry, I was now sad. It seemed like my words were falling on deaf ears with Colson.

"I know my beliefs may sound strange to you, but I feel like people create their own experiences, in their own lives and I feel it works generationally, too. If you're raised with a certain mindset that comes with certain expectations and it's hard to break out of," Colson was looking at me. My face must have betrayed how confusing I found his words to be.

"It's like this," he continued on. "Black people in America grow up hearing this narrative that White Americans feel they're better than us, they control the wealth, they control the media, they control the corporations...it becomes part of the collective psyche. Do you know how hard it is to release all of that negative energy? Whites in this country are also brought up with a narrative that they control everything, so believing that, they go out into the world and they control everything."

"A lot of that is true, though," I stated.

"It may be true, now, but by putting so much attention on that, it will only continue to be true. Our thoughts create our reality."

I found his words mystifying. I started to wonder if he was 100 percent sane. I began to gather up my things to leave. I had only wanted to eat my lunch in silence, just as I had every other day. *Why had he been waiting outside of my class anyway? Was it his aim to annoy me?*

"Why are you leaving?" he asked. "I apologize if I made you uncomfortable. I usually don't share my thoughts with people, because I know many aren't ready to hear them."

"*'Aren't ready to hear them'*? No, I'm not *ready* to hear words that aren't true. Those people who died in Katrina, and who die each day in this country or suffer due to inequality don't *create that reality* with their thoughts. The system in this country was never intended to serve them." This was the most I had ever said to Colson.

"Can we change the subject?" Colson asked. "I honestly didn't mean to offend you." Part of me still wanted to leave, but I believed that he didn't mean to offend me.

"Why were you outside Dr. Bryan's class, anyway?" I asked.

"I was waiting for you," he replied nonchalantly. "You mentioned you were in his class. My roommate is taking it, too." I didn't remember ever saying that. He rubbed his hands over his curly afro and then rubbed them together. "Anaya, I want to get to know you better..." he stopped there. He looked at me intently with his honey colored eyes. It was then that I noticed that they had specks of green near his iris. As he tried to make eye contact with me, I looked down. Somehow his words had an effect on me. My body suddenly felt warm. He always seemed to have a way of making me uncomfortable. His words and actions made me feel unbalanced in a strange way, but he also interested me. I had never met anyone like him before. Yet, I knew being friends with him was out of the question.

"I don't have male friends," I said. I gathered my bag and got up from the table. He looked at me oddly. "You're leaving?" It was as if he was the one questioning my sanity now.

"Yes, I'm leaving. I appreciate you tutoring me and everything, Colson, but I think it's best if we keep it at that." I walked away before he had the chance to reply.

Chapter 6

Looking back, it still shocks me to think about how very serious I was during that time in my life. After walking away from Colson that day, I can remember feeling as though I was Lut leaving the city of Gomorrah, resolved to never look back. Everything was so black and white to me at that time. I compartmentalized things into columns: good or bad, halal[15] or haram. Anything that didn't fit into one of those boxes agitated me.

The next morning, I walked from the bus stop to the morning shift at the library in a literal and figurative haze. It had rained the night before, yet the heat of the sun blazed upon the concrete from dawn. The effect was a balmy steam that rose from the asphalt. It was a shimmering fog that floated amongst the trees, and made me feel as if I was in a dream.

---

[15] Halal: permitted. Haran: not permitted.

I was at an intellectual impasse. Many times, I was told that men and women were not supposed to be alone together or be friends unless they were married or related. Yet, deep inside I knew that my treatment towards Colson had been rude and cold.

Approaching the library, I saw Zayna sitting on one of the concrete benches out front. She had on headphones and was reading a textbook. Her thick dark hair was covered loosely by a taupe colored shawl. I had a few minutes before my shift began, so I was happy to see her.

"You just walked away from him?" she asked. Her laughter echoed in the fog. I had told her about my interaction with Colson the day before.

"Yes, I walked away. I couldn't believe he said that!" I replied. I wasn't laughing along with her.

She stopped laughing and looked at me intently. "What are you scared of?" she asked. Her question made me feel unsettled.

"I'm not scared of anything," I replied. "I just know it's not appropriate for us to be friends, and he makes me feel a little uncomfortable."

She shrugged. "I don't know, Anaya, it seems impossible in this society, in these times, for you to never interact or be friendly with a guy. And I know that's the way your parents raised you, but what about someone like me? I have to work. I can't put a wall up. I sometimes ask male classmates for notes when I have to miss a class. Is all that *haram*?" The way she said *haram* was as if it was a bad word. She narrowed her eyes as the term came out of her lips. "I really don't see the big deal. I think Allah judges us on our character and our intentions as well as our actions."

Zayna's words stayed with me throughout the day. I started to question myself: *what exactly was I scared of?* I wasn't sure. I just knew that Colson made me feel off balance. At the same time his ideas fascinated yet frustrated me. I wanted to know more about his views on life, but I also wanted to run away. One minute I was resolved to apologize to him and another I wanted to run right to the foreign language office and ask to be removed from the tutoring program altogether. Like the fog that had settled around me that morning, my thoughts about him were unclear, hazy, and unfocused.

I decided to channel my feelings into my school work. I had an essay due in Dr. Bryan's class. That afternoon, I wrote nearly nonstop. I quoted James Baldwin and Audre Lorde. I compared media images of Emmett Till to those of victims of the levee collapse. I wrote about "Post Traumatic Slave Syndrome" and the "Prison Industrial Complex." These were terms that I had learned in my readings. The ideas were fascinating to me, and helped me look at the world in a new way. In the back of my mind was my discussion with Colson. It included everything I had really wanted to say to him, and all my thoughts that I had been holding back in class. When I was done, my essay was nearly twenty pages.

I returned home that evening to find my mother sitting at the kitchen table waiting for me. She sat upright in the chair, reading Qur'an silently to herself. She wore her emerald green "house" abaya, the one she wore more often than not. It had a few faded patches and threadbare spots, yet she refused to stop wearing it. It was a memento from her and my father's trip to Hajj many years ago. The abaya was as familiar to me as my mother's hesitant smile.

"Anaya, I've been trying to call you," she said sternly. On her face was a disapproving look. One I had seen many times as she scolded Sadiya.

"I didn't realize..." I found my phone in my pocket. The battery died. "I'm sorry, Mommy. I didn't know the battery was dead." I tried to give her a hug, yet her body stiffened.

"Why are you home so late? Doesn't your last class end at three today?" she asked. It was 6pm.

"Yes, but I have a paper due on Monday. I was in the computer lab finishing it." Even though my words were true and I hadn't been doing anything wrong, the disapproving look stayed upon my mother's face. She sighed deeply.

"Mama, it's the truth. I can show you the paper if you want."

She shook her head. "That's between you and Allah, Anaya." She adjusted the black scarf that covered her cornrowed hair. "I know you're a good girl, but you have to remember, Shaytan works hard to get us to go astray. Now you're at that school with all those non-Muslims. You have to stay vigilant. Don't let the whisperings of the Shaytan throw you off course," she went on.

"Remember what the Qur'an says Anaya, 'Shaytan promises them and entices them; what the devil promises is no more than an illusion.'" With these words she left the kitchen table and returned to her room.

I could feel hot tears stinging my eyes. Since starting school, I had done nothing except go straight to class or the library and return home. I shied away from interacting with almost everyone unless it was directly related to class. I had avoided the student lounge, and I dared not even ask to attend any of the basketball games or club activities. Yet, it still wasn't enough.

That night, I went to sleep filled with frustration. I wondered if I would ever be able to truly please my parents. I thought about what Zayna had said, was it even possible to uphold the standards that they had for me?

The next week was spring break, and I was grateful for the week off to just relax and reflect on everything. Writing the essay for Dr. Bryan's class had felt like a relief. There had been so many ideas that I had left unexpressed since the beginning of the semester. Getting all of those thoughts out finally, felt like a cleansing for the part of my mind that had been held in for far too long. I was also beginning to see the situation with Colson with fresh eyes. I now felt that I had been rude and I wanted to apologize to him. I was beginning to realize that staying in my box wasn't really an option anymore. Maybe being so staunch was only holding me back. From not speaking up in French class to never raising my hand in Dr. Bryan's class to snubbing people who could help me— perhaps I was preventing myself from getting the most out of being in college.

Of course, I knew in my heart the ultimate goal was to please Allah. I still didn't plan on doing anything that went against my morals. Yet were all the extra restrictions that my parents imposed really necessary? These were the thoughts that were on my mind throughout the break.

That week was also the week of the masjid's annual beautification project. It was an annual event where we invited the community to assist in revitalizing the masjid. Each day had a different task to be completed in and outside of the facility. Volunteers from other mosques also attended helping with tasks like painting, planting flowers, cleaning the carpets and rugs, pulling weeds from the garden in the backyard and preparing the garden plots for my mother, who planted a vegetable garden there each spring.

This was the only time, outside of Ramadan, that the masjid also had nightly dinners to thank the many volunteers who helped with the project. I was on kitchen duty that week, although I would have preferred to be painting or helping with the landscaping. Those teams seemed to be having fun, working together and talking while they did their jobs. From the window in the kitchen, I could hear the chatter and an occasional burst of laughter from them.

My mother proudly displayed her nightly menu on a placard outside of the kitchen. She really loved Masjid Beautification Week. She was humming and floating through the small kitchen as she chopped this and stirred that.

My father was all over the masjid, talking with the different teams, welcoming the volunteers, and offering a few good words here and there. Besides teaching Islamic studies classes, Sister Qadira was also known for her bottled sorrel. It was a red drink made from hibiscus leaves, flavored with ginger and lemon. She sweetened it with honey and bottled it up to distribute. One particular afternoon she arrived with her car loaded with coolers filled with the drink.

"Anaya, would you mind helping me pass out my sorrel?" she asked after greeting my mother with hugs and *salams*. She wore a large straw hat over her white *hijab.* Her long flowing dress nearly touched the ground. Her hug felt familiar like that of a family member and she smelled of honey and ginger.

I was grateful to leave my duty in the kitchen and quickly removed my apron. I wore a long black maxi dress with a print of small pink flowers. I had pinned my pink cotton *hijab* in place carefully that morning so that it framed my face. I was becoming more aware of clothing and fashion. I had chosen the outfit carefully so that I felt confident in, yet it wasn't something my parents would disapprove of. I followed Sister Qadira out to the car. Her coolers were on wheels, and I was able to roll one to the front porch of the masjid and began passing out the bottles.

The volunteers took this as an opportunity to take a break and they milled around under the trees in the masjid courtyard. The masjid was already looking refreshed from the work everyone had done so far. They had scraped off years of paint from the exterior and were now repainting the outside with beige siding and green trim. The front yard now had flowers planted, surrounded by mulch and the back deck had been power washed, and looked almost like new.

The masjid was gleaming from all of the effort. The energy of the yard was happy and filled with a hopeful spirit. It wasn't often the place was filled with so many familiar and new faces. Even people who hadn't come to the masjid in months were there, including some of the girls who had stopped coming to weekend classes.

My father was under a tree talking to a group of young brothers. Some looked familiar, and there were new faces in that group as well. I gave my salams and began passing out drinks.

"Brothers, this is my daughter. Anaya, some of these young men attend Xavier University. I was telling them that they should come out here more often," I nodded in their direction and looked down. It felt uncomfortable to have so many eyes on me.

"What do you study?" one of them asked. I glanced up to see him looking at me keenly. He was only a little bit taller than me and had a short beard which he played with twisting a few of the hairs with his left hand.

"My major is education," I replied, looking down.

"Oh really? Mine is electronic engineering, but yours is much more important to society."

I nodded, unsure of what to say. I had spent all day wanting to come outside, but now that I was, retreating back to the comfort of the kitchen seemed like a good idea.

"I guess both are needed," I finally replied.

"I see your mother finally let you out of the kitchen," my father said, as if he was reading my thoughts. "I pray that you young brothers can stay for dinner. My wife and Anaya have been working hard preparing everything. Insha Allah you all can stay and partake with us."

I looked up to see the young men nodding. The one who had asked me about my major, was still glancing my way occasionally. His jeans were worn out and faded, and he had on a plain gray t-shirt and stiff looking leather sandals. I gave my *salams* and continued to the other groups, passing out Sister Qadira's drinks.

The fence was being repainted by a group of girls that had once attended Sister Qadira's classes regularly. I gave my hugs and greetings. One, named Suhaila was a few years older than me. I hadn't seen her since two Ramadans ago. "I hear you're in college now?" she asked.

I nodded. "How about you?" I asked. She didn't have on *hijab*, but she wore a thin blue scarf casually draped around her neck. Later, she would use it to cover her hair quickly when it was time for prayers. Her curly hair had been arranged carefully into two French braids.

"I'm almost done, insha Allah this will be my last semester at Dillard," she replied with a smile. I was surprised to hear this. Usually my father put all of the names of the students who were graduating in the newsletter, asking for prayers for their success. She said that she was studying pre-Law and would be continuing on to Law School at Tulane. We exchanged numbers and we agreed to meet up over the break.

I completed passing out the sorrel just as the *adhan* for Maghrib[16] Prayer was being called. The voice over the loudspeaker calling everyone to prayer wasn't that of Brother Abdul-Hakim, who usually had the task. As I went inside to prepare for prayer, I wondered who Brother Abdul-Hakim had allowed to call it in his place. The voice was strong yet soft and he paused slightly between each verse. His *adhan*[17] was clear and reminded me of the call to prayer from Medina that I had heard many times on my mother's adhan clock at home. As I entered the prayer hall, I could see the student who had asked me about my major was finishing up the adhan. I would never have guessed that his adhan would have sounded like that.

After the Maghrib Prayer, I returned to my post in the kitchen. I was "working the line." We arranged all the food on long tables, and myself and some other teenagers had the responsibility of serving as each person went down the row. My mother refused to allow anyone to serve himself on her watch.

People began to line up with their empty plates, ready for them to be filled. Tonight, they had a choice of fried fish or baked chicken, dirty rice or seafood pasta, potato salad or corn on the cob, and finally green salad

---

[16] The prayer made at sunset.
[17] The Islamic call to prayer.

or one made with just cucumbers and tomatoes. My mother had given us strict orders on how much of each item to put on each person's plate, there was also no wasting on her watch. I was on potato salad duty, putting one scoop on each person's plate, as I had done so many times in the past. Sadiya had arrived just before the Maghrib Prayer and landed the easy job—salad duty. She didn't have to worry about anyone trying to convince her to pile an extra helping of salad onto their plate.

I settled into the monotony of the job. I laughed at the jokes that the men my father's age and older made year after year. I gave *salams* to the women and girls that I knew. Some didn't say anything, they simply filled their plate and moved on. The hard work in the hot sun had exhausted many of the volunteers and they seemed grateful for the food, cold bottles of water, and air conditioning in the dining hall. I was almost out of potato salad, when I looked up to see the same young man who had called the *adhan*. He was looking at me intently again, and I shifted my weight on my feet, looking down at the nearly empty aluminum dish.

"Would you like some potato salad?" I asked. He wasn't holding his plate out like most people had, nor was he making an attempt at conversation. He was just standing there focused on me. The line was nearly empty, almost all the volunteers were seated at the round tables in the hall eating and chatting.

He cleared his throat before finally replying. "Yes, thank you." I began to scoop the potato salad onto his plate. "How do you like it at UNO?" he asked. I wasn't expecting him to try and make conversation.

"It's ok, alhamdulillah[18]. It's a big school, so it's different for me," I replied.

"Oh really? Did you go to a small high school?"

"Actually, I was homeschooled." He raised his eyebrows. My back was hurting from all the cooking and serving. I was ready to take off my apron, have a seat, and finally enjoy whatever food my mother had stashed away for me in the kitchen. I was trying to be nice, yet I wondered why he insisted on making conversation right now.

"Well, Anaya, my name is Jahid. I hope to see you around. Your father invited me to his Saturday class, so maybe I'll see you then," with these words he moved on. I watched as he walked to the table where his friends, the other Xavier students, were sitting. They watched him expectantly as he approached.

I have thought a lot about this day. I have wondered what would have happened if Jahid hadn't come to the masjid that day. Or if I was sick or too tired, and wasn't there myself. On the surface, it seems like the most pivotal moments in our lives appear so happenstance, yet I know in my heart that they are

---

[18] All Praise due to God.

carefully arranged by the Creator of all that is in the heavens and on earth.

I didn't think anything of my meeting with Jahid in that moment. I had no idea that moment held more weight than perhaps anything that had occurred in my life up to that point.

Chapter 7

When I look back at the young woman I was at that time in college, it confuses me where all of my self-consciousness and anxiety came from. Yes, I grew up in a sheltered environment, but so did girls like my sister and Suhaila. They didn't have that same fear within them. And what was I afraid of? So many things...if life is a game, I was afraid of losing or failing, yet I was also afraid of winning and calling attention to myself. I was told by my parents and Sister Qadira that a Muslim woman shouldn't call attention to herself. Yet I was in a lose-lose situation. I was slowly, but surely beginning to realize that.

When I returned to school, after Spring Break, I was surrounded with conversations about other students' trips to close-by beaches, or even nightly excursions to Bourbon Street. When asked what I had done during my break, I spoke up. "We were having mosque beautification week and I helped out with that," I responded to a girl named Nicole in my Educational Psychology class. We had chatted before, but mainly to exchange notes. This was the first time we had actually shared any personal information.

"Oh really? They have something like that at my church," she replied. She didn't look surprised to hear about my activities during the break, in fact she seemed interested. She asked a few questions about the event and the mosque itself. I soon realized that so much of my fear came from overthinking casual situations, and I promised myself to stop letting my mind reflect on all the ways things could go wrong, and instead accept situations as they are.

The next class of the day was Dr. Bryan's. As I walked up to the classroom, I could see Dr. Bryan at the lectern sorting through our papers. I remembered the essay I had written and turned in the day before our break began. I had hoped that I could earn a high enough grade to not have to do a revision. Dr. Bryan never gave out a failing grade, he only required students to rewrite their essays until their work was worthy of passing. I had heard stories of students who had to rewrite their essays three or more times until the work was good enough.

"I'd like to see the following students after class: Jeremy Williams, Vanessa Shaw, and Anaya Abdul Aziz,"

Dr. Bryan stated. He then cleared his throat and began his lecture. My mind was racing, I wondered how my essay could have been bad enough to require a revision. I attempted to pay attention to the lecture, which was about the origin of rap. "The tradition of rap is directly related to the West African Griot tradition that we spoke about at the beginning of the semester. We know that Griots used their highly poetic rhetorical forms to glorify or condemn community members, however they also used it to carry news and generational stories and fables, so we can see that this is not so different than the original rap groups that saw rise in the late 1960s," Dr. Bryan lectured.

I tried to focus on Dr. Bryan's words, and take notes, but my mind wandered back to my essay and what could have been wrong with it. What I remember most about. Dr. Bryan was his deep voice that seemed to fill every corner of the classroom, and demand the attention of even the disinterested students. The resonance of his voice was not enough to keep my attention that day. Dr. Bryan was a tall man. His smooth dark skin lacked any wrinkles, even though his black hair was speckled with gray. He also had a salt and pepper beard, which he tugged on from time to time. I imagined standing before him, in my mind he would tear apart my paper as his thundering voice echoed throughout the classroom.

Finally, the lecture was over and the other two students Dr. Bryan had called approached his lectern. I purposely took my time finishing some notes, and packing up my bag before going to the front of the room. I didn't want to talk to him in front of everyone and I wanted to have more time with him to hear his tips on how to improve my essay.

After Jeremy and Vanessa left the room, I approached Dr. Bryan. "You asked to see me. I'm Anaya," I began.

"Yes, Anaya...I did want to talk to you. Your essay, it just blew me away. It is phenomenal." I took a deep breath. *Phenomenal?*

"So, you liked it?" I asked.

"Of course. You know as a professor, I try to teach students how to fully understand and grasp what they've learned in class, yet I also want them to challenge themselves. Ideally, I want students to relate what they've learned in class to other circumstances, to reach outside of class so to speak," Dr. Bryan took my essay out of a manila folder and I could see the A+ written across the top. My mind was racing, if Dr. Bryan liked my essay, why did he want to speak with me?

"I wanted to ask you, what is your major? The reason I'm asking is, I have some great opportunities coming up for History and Africana Studies majors. Based on your writing, I feel confident that we could secure you scholarships and publishing opportunities." Dr. Bryan looked excited as he relayed this information to me. I listened to his words. I had never thought about majoring in History and Africana Studies. I had never even heard of it until coming to college. I wondered what could you do with one of those majors.

"I'm majoring in Education," I replied. I had come to school to finish my degree as quickly as possible, obtain my teaching license, and begin teaching at a school. In my mind, there could be no better way for me to contribute to society. Could a historian make the same impact as a teacher?

"Have you ever thought about majoring in History or Africana Studies and minoring in Education? You could still teach in schools, but like I said, you could also get some scholarships, publish some of your essays...there are even some great travel opportunities." Dr. Bryan ruffled through his laptop bag and came out with a few brochures and pamphlets about the school's History and Africana Studies programs as well as a few about study abroad opportunities in places like Morocco and Senegal.

"I've never really considered switching majors, but it sounds interesting," I said. I looked at the pamphlets. What excited me most was the scholarships that could help pay for my books and other incidentals that my grant and work study money hadn't covered. I knew it had been a heavy burden for my parents to purchase my books the last two semesters. The text for Dr. Bryan's class alone had been over $100.

"Well, I want you to consider it now," he said with a chuckle. "Please think about it and meet with me during my office hours, so that we can discuss everything." I agreed to think about everything and go over the materials he had given me, but in my heart, I knew I had already made my decision. I would be switching my major to History.

That afternoon, I was supposed to meet with Colson for tutoring and I wondered if he would even show up considering how rude I had been the last time that I saw him. As I approached the study carrel where we usually met, I realized he was already there. He had his afro hidden in a backwards cap and was reading from a small book.

"Hi...uh Salut," I said after taking a deep breath. "I wanted to apologize to you...I think I was rude the last time we spoke," I had been practicing my speech for a few days. In my mind I knew exactly what I was going to say to him, yet the words seemed to deteriorate now that he sat looking at me silently.

He shrugged slightly. "I was doing some reading, and I understand your reaction now. I guess you're not supposed to have male friends...I never knew that. Your religion... it interests me. I never really had a Muslim friend before, not one that practiced anyway. It intrigues me."

Now that I was seated, I could see what Colson was reading. The title was "A Brief Illustrated Guide to Understanding Islam." I had seen the small book countless times. My father bulk ordered them and kept copies in his office for non-Muslim visitors. I wasn't expecting for Colson to be reading it.

"What made you decide to read that?" I asked. The cover of the book was so familiar to me. It featured a drawing of the galaxy, the rings and spirals formed by the stars and planets of our solar system had always been a reminder for me that none of this could have been created haphazardly. None if it was an accident.

"My major is Comparative Religion. Learning about different beliefs interests me," he said placing the book back into his bag. I would never have guessed he was any type of theology major. Most of the theology majors on our campus were preparing to be in a religious order of one kind or another.

"Do you follow one?" I asked. I prepared myself to be surprised again. Maybe he was a devout Christian for all I knew.

"No. I consider myself agnostic," he replied. I guess he saw the confusion on my face. "I believe in a Creator, but I don't follow one set of rules or one particular religion. To me, there's some truth in them all," he continued. I wondered what an agnostic planned to do with a degree in Comparative Religion, but I didn't ask. I had enough on my mind to process for one day.

"Well, anyway," he continued, "I know there's a limit to how much you would allow me to get to know you, but I would like to get to know you better, outside of tutoring." He closed the book, and placed it into his messenger bag.

"Why?" I asked. "Why do you want to know me?" I wondered why he was so adamant about us forging a friendship.

"Honestly, you interest me. Like I said, I've never really known a Muslim before, and it's not just that, you just seem cool. You act like you don't know just how fly you are," he finished, removing his cap and running his hands through his curly fro. That was the first time anyone had used the word "fly" to describe me. I didn't know how to react, and so I simply shrugged and began taking out my textbooks instead of saying anything.

We spent the remainder of the hour studying from my textbook and completing my homework assignment. Even though I wasn't sure about a friendship with Colson, I was grateful for his help in French. Without his assistance, I might have failed that semester. As our session drew to a close, I decided to tell Colson about my paper.

"Remember our conversation the day before break? I ended up writing a whole paper about it," I began.

"Oh really? I'm not surprised you seemed really passionate about the topic," he laughed. "I don't remember the last time I saw someone so amped up," he said jokingly.

"Well, I guess I should thank you, because Dr. Bryan loved the essay and he wants me to consider switching my major to History or Africana studies. He said I could get a scholarship or maybe even money to travel abroad."

Colson raised his eyebrows. "Wow, so are you going to do it?"

"I think I will. I didn't realize how much I love to read and research topics like this, and I could still minor in Education and get my teaching license."

"If you major in African-American History, you should go on to get a PhD. Write books. Give lectures. There are plenty of teachers in elementary and high schools already. You could shape minds and teach in a different way."

I thought about Colson's words. The thought of me lecturing and writing books seemed crazy, and yet the idea fascinated me. Would anyone want to hear what I had to say?

"Dr. Bryan liked your paper enough to recommend that you switch majors. That's huge," Colson stated. "Someday teachers in the classroom will be instructing from your books." I allowed his words to settle upon me like a blanket. I liked the warmth and the weight of them, and they provided comfort to me on that day, and on many days in the future I would invoke those words again and find peace in the warmth and gentle pull of them.

73

That day, I agreed to be friends with Colson. I saved his number in my phone simply as "French Tutor."

It was the first time I had ever done anything intentionally that I knew my parents would disapprove of. Yet, I told myself it was all innocent, and it was. I enjoyed talking to Colson and our debates provided me lots to ponder. He challenged my thinking in a way that no one else had. When I told Zayna about our friendship, she brushed it off as no big deal. She was much more interested in me changing my major, and the possible opportunities it could bring me. We filled out the forms required to change majors and looked at all of the materials Dr. Bryan had given me.

"You should definitely apply for some of these," she said while flipping through the study abroad opportunities. We sat on the floor of her apartment, sipping on mugs of hot tea, as had become our tradition on afternoons when neither of us was working or in class. The sparse furnishings in the room had become very familiar to me. The futon was lumpy and uncomfortable, so we usually sat on the floor. Zayna had a few decorative cushions which we could sit on. Her coffee table was usually covered in her textbooks and her laptop. Her prayer garment was folded neatly in the corner on top of her lush purple prayer rug, which was also folded meticulously.

The photos in one particular brochure looked persuasive. It showed students interviewing writers and historians in Morocco. The photographs highlighted the country's architecture which featured geometric designs on doors and floors, and huge mosques with staggering minarets. There were even photos of the food, with tantalizing platters of couscous, vegetables, and legs of lamb. I imagined myself in the scene, afterall, I knew a little Arabic and thanks to Colson, my French was improving. Both languages would be useful in Morocco. I pictured myself living at the University of Fez for a semester, praying in those stunning mosques, studying Moroccan history and eating from platters of couscous with my bare hands. The thought seemed tempting, but I knew it would be nearly impossible to convince my parents.

"You never know," Zayna said. "Maybe you could convince them if you explain how much you would experience there. It would be an unbelievable opportunity." I knew it would be amazing to be in Morocco soaking in all that culture, yet I also knew that my parents would never agree to me travelling alone without a *mahrem*. Still, I entertained the thought.

What was at the forefront of my mind, though, was explaining to my parents why I was switching my major from Education to History. I still planned to minor in Education and obtain my teaching license, but I hoped that they wouldn't think being in college was influencing me too much, that the environment was making me lose sight of my goals.

At the end of the day, my worries were unfounded. Later that evening, I explained to my mother that switching would make finding a teaching job easier, and she seemed unphased by the news. I didn't even have to mention my essay, Dr. Bryan or the scholarship opportunities. I didn't know it at the time, but my mother's mind was on other matters concerning my future.

Chapter 8

Something was going on with Sadiya that spring. It had been going on for several months. Neither of my parents came out and explained anything to me at the time, yet I could see the relationship between them and my sister was even more strained than usual. For months, I could hear their whispered discussions mentioning her name late into the night. Part of me wanted to know what it was all about, and part of me ignored it. I had always hated confrontation and avoided it at all costs.

However, I did wonder what she could be doing now that would cause so much turmoil. As a middle schooler, Sadiya had refused to be homeschooled any longer. Despite my mother's insistence, she simply stopped doing the work. So, she was enrolled in a public charter school.

As a teen, she stopped wearing the long dark colored *hijabs* that my parents required. Instead she opted for printed turbans or, much to my parents' dismay, nothing covering her head at all. After finishing high school, she moved out of the house. It didn't surprise me when I saw her collecting her things into bags and boxes, yet it did sadden me. I knew that she felt suffocated in our parents' home.

My sister is intensely artistic, and always has been. As a teen her walls were covered with everything from graffiti style graphics to charcoal portraits. All of these were done with her own hands and very little training. Her creativity was also reflected in her clothing and jewelry. She just wasn't the type to wear the dark colored *abayas* that my mother encouraged. Even the long skirts and tops I wore felt stifling to her. She lived and breathed color. Secretly, I loved her African print headwraps, wooden earrings, braided leather chokers, and her nails which she painted in shades of deep plum or maroon. Yet, the more she expressed herself, the more my parents disapproved. This had been going on so long that I would've thought they'd come to terms with the fact that Sadiya was going to live on her own terms. So, what had happened to upset them now?

I eventually found out from Sister Qadira, who didn't realize she was saying anything I didn't already know. It was after Sunday classes and I was helping her rearrange the small classroom. As we cleaned the dry erase boards and replaced Qur'ans on the small bookshelf, Sister Qadira patted my shoulder slightly. "I know your family has been hit with some trying times lately. You know the Shaytan is always working," she began. I shrugged. I hadn't pressed my parents about what was going on. Now, I was starting to think that maybe I should have.

"I've known you and Sadiya since Allah brought y'all to this planet," she said with a smirk. "Now, your sister has made some bad choices, I guess this one has to be the worst... her living with that boy, Dreaux...she's the one that's going to have to answer for that. Don't let her decisions make you feel ashamed about yourself." *Living with that Dreaux? No wonder my parents were so upset.*

I had known Dreaux for some time. Yet, I knew him as a friend of a friend of my sister. I had no idea their relationship went beyond that. He wasn't Muslim. They weren't married. Yet they were living together? This was bad.

"You know the Qur'an says, 'Whoever goes right, then he goes right only for the benefit of his own self. And whoever goes astray, then he goes astray to his own loss. No one laden with burdens can bear another's burden.' I tried telling your mother that," with these words Sister Qadira shrugged. "I'll just keep ya'll in my prayers and don't stop praying for Sadiya. Allah might see fit to bring her back to her right mind, just be patient. *Sabr, sabr, sabr.*[19]" With this, Sister

Qadira gave me one of her warm hugs and gathered her purse to leave.

I sat in one of the chairs in the classroom and thought about everything Sister Qadira had just said. I knew Sadiya well enough to know that she was going to do what she wanted, and trying to talk her out of it would only push her further away. I knew there was nothing I could do to convince her of anything. I decided to follow Sister Qadira's advice and make dua[20] for her. She had made her decision and she would have to live with it, whatever the outcome might be.

The next day, I was excited to return to school. I had filled out all of the paperwork to switch majors and I had a meeting with Dr. Bryan so that we could go over what classes I should take in the upcoming semester.

Dr. Bryan's office was like a tiny museum. It featured photos, books, and artifacts concerning many of the events we had spoken about in class and so many more. I wondered what I could find in the pages of books with titles like *Woman, Race, & Class, Black Skins, White Masks,* and *The Fire Next Time.* He had photos of himself with Dr. Cornel West and Dr. Frances Cress-Welsing. I tried to focus on his words, but it was difficult. My eyes kept darting to titles of books on his shelves and his photos. Thankfully, Dr. Bryan had a form in which he was writing the courses I should take during the

---

[19] Sabr: patience.
[20] Prayer

summer and fall. He suggested I take two classes over the summer, one math to complete my requirements and a history course titled *The Emancipation of Slavery in North and South America*. In the fall he suggested I take a few literature and history courses, including one with him.

"You know, Anaya, next Spring I'm leading a study abroad trip to Morocco," Dr. Bryan said, after handing me the form. I nodded. "Have you considered applying? There are some scholarships still available."

"I think it would be a great experience, but I'm not sure if my parents would allow me to go so far away by myself," I replied. I had actually never traveled alone. With everything that was going on with Sadiya, I wondered if I ever would.

"Well, it's an excellent opportunity. You can self-study and earn up to twelve credits towards your major."

"Self-study?" I had never heard the term before.

"Yes, you would come up with a topic for a research paper. During your stay in Morocco, you would research and write the essay using the resources available there. You have four weeks after returning to complete the essay, and after presenting it to a panel, you would earn your twelve credits," Dr. Bryan looked at me with his kind eyes. He made it sound so easy. "Why don't we just fill out the application and see how

81

it goes? When you get accepted, I'll talk to your parents myself. Maybe I could allay some of their fears."

"When I get accepted?" I asked. Dr. Bryan winked at me.

As we filled out yet another form, I wondered if my parents would allow me to take the trip. I thought maybe if Dr. Bryan talked to them, agreeing to act as my guardian while we were there, maybe they would accept. Part of me felt it was only wishful thinking, and part of me grew excited about the prospect. The possibility of being so far away from home and experiencing something that was so different scared and excited me.

That afternoon, as I shelved books in the library, I put a few books about Morocco onto my cart, reading a few pages whenever I had the chance. As I pushed the gray cart through stacks of books, my mind was occasionally transported to the country. The history of the country fascinated me, I learned about the Berbers and the Tuaregs, but the photos of the architecture attracted me, too. I imagined myself walking down the stone paved streets in the narrow alleys surrounded by those geometric tile designs and Islamic calligraphy. It seemed like another world.

As I got ready to clock out for the day, I was checking out a few of the books and realized I had a text message from *French Tutor*.

"Switch majors yet? How'd it go?" he asked. I hadn't seen or texted Colson since our last tutoring session.

"Yup! Applying for a scholarship for Morocco!" I replied.

"Cool! At Cafe YAYA. Wanna meet up?" Cafe YAYA was another space on campus that I hardly ever visited. It was a place where students met up to chat or study over coffee. I usually prefered the quiet of the library or the sofa at Zayna's apartment over the cafe, but I agreed to meet with him and promised myself that I would only stay for a little while. I wanted to catch the bus home before it was too late.

Walking into the packed cafe, I had a hard time spotting Colson. YAYA was filled with students staring into laptops at the tables or sprawled on the mismatched sofas reading or talking. There were even a few students napping on the cushy chairs in the back. I finally spotted Colson seated at a small table, and he waved me over.

"So, you're applying to go to Morocco?" Colson asked as soon as I sat down. He was drinking an iced tea and had his cap on backwards again.

I explained that if I got accepted all of my fees would be covered by the school. I told him about Dr. Bryan's wink and my guess that it meant I would likely get accepted. I also told him about the credits I would earn if I got to go.

"It seems dope. Why do you sound hesitant about it?" His eyes bore through me. I took in a deep breath.

"It's my parents...I just wonder if they'll allow me to go without a *meh*...I mean without a guardian," I explained.

Colson, took off his cap, ran his hands over his head and put it back on. I noticed his curly fro was getting bigger. "It's so odd to me. I've been traveling by myself since I was thirteen or fourteen. Overseas to visit family in France, and I even traveled here from New York when I came to volunteer in high school."

I folded my hands across my chest. I had to remember that Colson's reality was so different from my own. It would always be hard for him to understand the limits that my parents put upon me, and how they were intended to protect me and not restrict me. My thoughts turned to Sadiya and how she had refused my parents' protection and the situation she was in now. I wondered how she could be happy having caused so much upheaval in the family, and how she could sleep at night knowing that Allah couldn't be happy with her.

"I've never traveled alone before," I replied simply. "It doesn't make any sense to stress over it now. I'll only take it seriously when I find out for sure."

"Well, I hope you can find a way to go. I think it would be great for you to experience traveling there." I smiled at this comment. The possibility still made me happy, and maybe I could work it out somehow. "Do you want anything to eat or drink?" Colson asked.

"I just want some water." I moved to get up from my seat, but Colson insisted on getting it for me.

"I gotchu," he said. "You can stay right there." I watched as he walked to the counter and came back with a bottle of water, plus a glass of ice and a straw. "I wasn't sure if you wanted a bottle or a glass," he said, placing both in front of me.

I thanked him, yet I felt uncomfortable with him bringing me the water. Even though it was only water, I had never been served by a man outside of my family before and it made me feel awkward. Still, I hesitantly opened the bottle and filled the glass with water. I took a few sips, trying to calm myself.

"You have flown before, haven't you?" he asked. At this question I nearly spat out my water.

"Of course, I've flown," I replied laughing. "I'm not Amish." I told him about trips to visit family in other states, and even flying to Toronto with my family when my father had been invited to speak at a conference one winter.

"So, I even have a passport," I said sarcastically.

"I'm sorry," he said. "I didn't mean anything...I was just curious." He looked at me intently. I looked down at the table. I played with the straw wrapper, twisting it in my fingers. Something about his gaze was making me feel self-conscious.

"I know," I said. "I'm not offended." I looked up at him, allowing the silence between us to speak for itself. I decided not to fight against it. I looked at him now. I was always intrigued by his face, which to me was a mix of African and European features. His light skin stood in opposition to his broad lips. His light-colored eyes contrasted his wide nose. It was a striking combination.

"That scarf looks nice on you," he said, breaking the silence. "Your...*hajib*," he said.

I laughed again, "It's called a *hijab*," I said pronouncing the Arabic slowly.

"*Hijab*..." he repeated after me. Mine today was a deep maroon cotton scarf, the frayed edges framed my face and I had managed to keep it in place with only one straight pin.

Suddenly, his hand had spanned the distance between us at the small table. He fingers covered mine. At that moment, I was too taken aback to move. I stared for a second at his cocoa butter skin against my deeper brown. The table was covered with the remnants of my straw wrapper. I had torn it into tiny pieces. The bits of paper were scattered like confetti in a chaotic pile around our hands. Suddenly, the warmth of his hand turned to a heat that felt sure to burn. I moved my hand away from his quickly. It had only been a moment, yet in that moment I understood that Colson didn't want just friendship as he had said in the beginning.

I could hear my pulse in my ears. I wanted to jump and run away from the situation. Yet, my legs wouldn't move. I was stuck in that spot. I took a moment to control my breath. It was something so small...perhaps it had even been an accidental pat.

"Colson, I..." I began yet I didn't know how to finish. Looking up at him I could see a whole novel in his eyes. Suddenly, I had the strength to get up. I picked up my bag. "I'm sorry, I have to go." I rushed out of the cafe disappointed in myself for ever agreeing to meet him.

I didn't know at the time, but as I sat with Colson my parents were having a meeting of their own. When I arrived home that day, I found my mother seated at the kitchen table. She sat waiting patiently for me to return home, in her house abaya, sipping on tea and reading.

"Assalam Alaikum, Anaya," she greeted me as I walked through the door. I gave her a hurried reply, hoping to be able to escape into my room and be left alone. My head was spinning with thoughts about Colson. I thought we could just be friends, but that afternoon proved that that wouldn't be possible. We hadn't said anything to each other. Technically no lines had been crossed, except for him touching my hand. Yet, it was clear that there was so much each of us desired to express, and that is what made me fearful. I wanted to go into my room and try to make sense of all these feelings I was having.

But my mother wasn't going to allow me to escape into my room that day. "Anaya, sit down for a minute," she said. I sighed slightly, and sat in the chair across from her. My heart was racing. Did my mother know about me meeting up with Colson? Maybe someone from the masjid had seen me at YAYA. My mother did mention the masjid that evening, but not in the way I feared.

"Your father and I had some visitors at the masjid today," she began. This wasn't unusual. It seemed like my father was always having visitors. Why did my mother want to discuss these visitors with me?

"One was that brother you met during the masjid beautification. He goes to Xavier University." My mother looked at me, searching my eyes for some recognition.

"Oh really?" I said with a shrug. I didn't really remember who she was talking about, and I was confused as to why she was bringing him up.

"Yes. You might remember him...his name is Jahid. He's studying engineering over there." Then I knew who she was referring to. I thought back to that week, remembering the brother named Jahid, and his awkward attempts at conversation. I nodded, hoping my mother would get to the point.

"He came over with his father," here she paused. I still didn't understand the significance of what she was saying. I simply nodded again, wondering when she would make it plain.

"He asked about you," she finally said. "Anaya, Jahid is looking to get married. He thinks ya'll might be a good match." Married? Suddenly, my heart was pounding again. I could feel myself start to sweat. Marriage at this point was the furthest thing from my mind. I was eighteen years old. My main goal at that time was to finish college. My mother's words terrified me. My mother could see that her words weren't met with joy.

"Anaya, calm down. We only want you two to get to know each other. If it doesn't work out, that's fine. At least give him a chance."

"Mother, I'm only eighteen. I just want to finish school first, and then maybe think about marriage and all that later."

"You'll be nineteen soon, Anaya, and no one is saying you have to get married right away or that you can't finish school. He's in school, too. Maybe ya'll could work it out, but at least Allah would be pleased with you," my mother looked down. I could see the sadness in her eyes.

"Sometimes I wonder if we had planned for Sadiya's future like this, maybe she wouldn't have fallen into this situation she's in." This was the first time my mother had mentioned Sadiya to me in a while. I could see that my mother blamed herself for Sadiya's decisions. Yet, in my mind, I couldn't see how my parents could have prevented it.

I didn't want to refuse my mother. When she told me that she had given Jahid my phone number, I simply accepted the fact that he would be calling me soon, to "get to know me." I couldn't help but think that all of this was a direct result of my behavior. In my mind, I thought Allah had orchestrated all of this to prevent me from slipping further away from the standards of morality that I had set for myself. I blamed myself for meeting with Colson and being too friendly with him. It had left me vulnerable and opened my heart to confusion and feelings that weren't right.

I knew I wanted to continue to study and learn, and perhaps find a way to travel abroad rather than get married. Yet I didn't want to disappoint my mother, nor did I want to make the same mistakes that Sadiya had. I didn't fight against the current. I allowed myself to be swept away by the waves.

Chapter 9

The semester was winding to a close. The cool spring days were behind us and the upper 90-degree temperatures were back. This only added to the sense of restlessness on campus. The campus bookstore's displays of caps, gowns, and tassels, reminded us all of how close, or far away, from our goals we all were. I studied for finals, went to my campus job, and returned home conscientiously. I didn't even visit Zayna, although I did miss our chats. I was determined to finish out the semester strongly. I was hoping to earn all As. I had raised my C in French to a high B, and if I could ace the final, I could earn an A in the course, too. It was important that I didn't waste a moment. The caps and gowns had an even stronger effect upon me. I visualized the moment when I would don those seemingly sacred items. I didn't want anything or anyone to stand in the way of it.

Neither of my parents had a degree. My mother had earned some credits at a community college before getting married, but never finished. My father called himself a student in the school of hard knocks, jokingly. Both of them stressed Islamic education over secular pursuits, and my mother had told me many times that no person had a ranking above another except in regards to their deeds. In the end we would all stand before Allah, and a college diploma wouldn't assist anyone on that day. Yet, I could tell that my parents were pleased with the fact that I was finishing up another semester of college. I heard my mother mention it to friends and family members over the phone. My father outright referred to me as, "My daughter, the college student," when introducing me to visitors at the masjid. It felt good to make my parents proud. However, I knew in my heart that even if they didn't notice my accomplishments, earning my degree was something that I needed and wanted for my own sake.

So, it was my own drive that forced me to stay up late into the night studying and editing essays. I even avoided my phone, unless it was to answer a call or text from my parents. I didn't respond to any of Colson's calls or texts. I did feel bad when he sent the final text, "Did I do something wrong?" After that one, I deleted his number. I felt a tinge of guilt for cutting him off so abruptly, but I had a deep knowledge that continuing our interactions just wasn't possible.

Then there was Jahid. He did call, as my mother had said he would. We had a few awkward conversations, in which he asked questions about my likes and dislikes. I posed the same questions back to him. He liked Indian food, and could read and write Arabic. I didn't know what to ask, so I let him lead the conversations. I was surprised to learn that he was ten years older than me, 28. I wondered why he was still in school at his age, but it felt like it would be rude to ask. He lived with his father and step-mother not far from Xavier. He worked in a shoe store in addition to being in school. I didn't know what to ask him. What could I ask him that carried enough weight? And would he be 100% honest anyway? I chose to listen instead. We spoke twice, before I told him I needed to focus on final exams, and he said he would call back in a week. So, I put him out of my mind, too.

During this time, the process of quietly reshelving books in the library became an enjoyable process. The silence of the library, the woodsy smell of the books, the sunlight filtering through the window blinds, and the soft creak of the wheels on my book cart put me in a nearly meditative state. My afternoons in the long stacks of books, were my most tranquil moments. On one of those quiet afternoons, as I pushed my cart through the stacks, I turned the corner to see Colson standing there. He stood so motionless that he appeared to be a vision. Seeing him made my heart race.

"I've been calling you," he whispered. I took a deep breath. I didn't really know what to say. I didn't want to deal with this conversation. Yet, I couldn't run from it this time. He had me cornered. He took a few quick steps forward and suddenly he was right in front of me. I struggled to catch my breath.

"Colson, I..." my mind was blank. My hands were on my cart, wanting to push it anywhere that wasn't near him.

"What are you afraid of?" He whispered softly into my ear. He placed his hands over mine, and removed them from the cart. I felt paralyzed. He was so close that I could feel his warm breath on my cheek. I was scared of him, and of the feelings that were consuming me in that moment. Yet, I said nothing. I took a deep breath, trying to get the momentum to move or even speak before things went too far. I felt hot all over. I wanted to run away from him and these feelings once and for all.

In an instant his lips brushed against my cheek. Before I could even make sense of the sensation, my hands were forcefully pushing him away. My heartbeat thumped in my ears. I pushed him so hard that his back hit my book cart. The clang of the metal cart coupled with the crash of books hitting the ground destroyed the peace of the 4th floor.

"I'm so sorry, Colson," I said. I wasn't sure if I was sorry for pushing him or forever allowing the situation to get to this point. What signs had I given him to let him think that his kiss upon my cheek would have been welcome? I took a few deep breaths and tried to gain control of myself.

All of it was enough for me to finally find the words I needed to say. I told him that I didn't like him in *that* way. I told him I didn't want him to tutor me anymore. I told me he had gotten the wrong idea. I lied. I don't want to remember the look on his face as I told him all of this. I knew I had done what I had to do, yet I knew that it was hurt in his eyes that I saw, and it mirrored the pain inside of me.

I rushed home from school, after leaving the library, and went straight to my room. My mother questioned me as to why I didn't want dinner. I vaguely complained of a stomach ache.

It was that night that I prayed for the feelings I had for Colson to dissolve. I knew from many years sitting in Sister Qadira's classes that one of my utmost duties as a Muslim woman was to lower my gaze and guard my modesty. I felt a depth of disappointment in myself that I hoped to never feel again.

Late into the night, with tears of contrition streaming down my cheeks, I begged for Allah's forgiveness and asked that he save me from going further astray than I already had. I knew that my feelings were a direct result of not following His commands and those of my parents. I knew I was never supposed to have a male tutor or allow myself to get overly friendly with him. In my mind, these feelings were a result of me transgressing bounds that were put in place only for my own protection. That night, I made supplication for Allah to protect me from going any further. I prayed for strength, and ultimately, I prayed for forgiveness and guidance.

The next day, I awoke to the bright sun shining through my window. I felt hopeful. My thoughts were again focused on putting everything that had happened with Colson behind me once and for all. I felt thankful that I hadn't allowed myself to be swept away by my feelings. I wouldn't end up making the same mistakes that my sister had made. I wouldn't commit the same wrongs that I had seen so many of the young girls I grew up with make over the years. The bright sun, for me, signified a new day. I had made an error, yet I felt hopeful. I had stopped myself before things had gotten too far. I could now refocus.

I dressed in a long floral maxi dress, and a light cardigan. With my dusty rose scarf pinned carefully into place, I felt ready to take my final exam of the semester. I had plans to sell back some of my books to the campus bookstore and check-in with the financial aid office to make sure the two summer classes I had planned to take were secured through my scholarship. Flash cards in my hands, my bookbag on my back, I came to the kitchen ready to face the day.

My mother sat waiting for me. "Good morning," I said. She had prepared two plates of eggs and toast, and she was already sipping on tea.

My mother greeted me with a smile. "Have some breakfast. You're always running in and out of here like it's a hotel," she said with a laugh.

"Ok, but I can't stay long. I have a final today and some errands at school to take care of," I pulled out a chair and sat down. I poked at the eggs and toast my mother had prepared. I looked up to see my mother's eyes resting intently upon me. I now knew that she had something to say. I rested my fork on my plate and looked at her expectantly.

"Jahid called your father yesterday," she finally said. "He really seems to like you." *Like me?* I wondered what he liked about me. We had barely spoken. I didn't know what to say, so I said nothing. "He asked about the prospect of marriage."

"Marriage? Mama, we've barely spoken. I don't really know him and he doesn't know me," I was having a hard time controlling the volume of my voice. I knew I was almost yelling, yet I couldn't help it.

"You young people are making marriage too complicated these days," she said. "We just want to protect you from making the same mistakes as your sister." My mother looked down with these words, not before I could still see the sadness in her eyes.

97

Her words gave me pause. Hadn't I prayed for the very same thing just last night? My heartbeat quickened as I remembered the prayers I had uttered just hours ago. I didn't want to make the same mistakes as my sister, or the ones I had seen so many of my classmates in Sister Qadira's class make. Yet, I didn't want to get married either. I thought of the shiny pamphlets for the study abroad program that were in my backpack. I thought of my goals of finishing school, and becoming a teacher or maybe even a professor. Would I have to sacrifice all of that in order for Allah to be pleased with me? I also thought of the sadness present in my mother's eyes. If I refused marriage, would I make the sadness in her eyes even more pronounced? My mouth felt dry, and I struggled to swallow. There was so much I wanted to say to her, that I couldn't. My entire body felt heavy. Suddenly I was very tired.

I didn't know what to say, so I said nothing. I sat at the table silently, and allowed my mother to speak.

Later that same day, I was again at a loss for words at the same table. My father and Jahid were also seated there. I played with my mother's floral embroidered placemats, and said nothing for a long time. Looking back, I realize it was fear mixed with awe that kept me from expressing myself fully.

I tried to understand how all of this had come about. I looked down at Jahid's stiff sandals. My parents sat close together. My father posed a few questions, while my mother nodded at the answers. They both looked pleased.

Jahid spoke about his studies in school. He spoke about his plans to secure an apartment close to his school. My parents then asked if we wanted a few moments of privacy to speak to each other. I again said nothing, but Jahid answered. "I think that would be nice," he said. My parents rose from the table and went into the living room. They left the kitchen door open, so we weren't really alone.

It was at this time that I finally looked up. He had a thin beard that needed a trim. He wore a white knit kufi and a polo shirt. I looked at his cocoa brown skin, and finally I looked into his eyes. There were so many questions that I wanted to ask. Yet, how could I know he would be honest? I took a deep breath. I saw kindness in his brown eyes. I thought about the fact that Allah had orchestrated all of this. Perhaps it would be best to simply trust in Allah and allow it all to unfold.

So instead of asking any questions, I said. "I want to finish my studies and I don't want to have children right away." He looked at me incredulously. Had I been too blunt?

He then let out a laugh. I liked the tone of his laughter and the way he threw his head back and allowed the waves of laughter to flow over and through him.

"Of course, you can finish school. I should be with an educated woman. We don't have to have kids right away, either," he finished. He played with his facial hair. He had a scar near his right temple, which I later learned was from a childhood accident. He had been running, and slipped on a puddle of water which his brother had spilled, hitting his head on the hard tile floor. He told me about the blood that gushed forth from the wound, and the stitches that had to be put in at the emergency room. Even then, I thought it a shame that one person's mistake could have such a lasting effect upon another.

Sitting at the table that day, I made a decision to trust in Allah's plan. I wanted to please my parents and my creator, that's true. Yet, I also hoped that marrying Jahid would be a part of my happy ending. I imagined marrying him, finishing my degree, and eventually teaching. I hoped that he would allow me to study in Morocco. I pictured us having children someday. In my visions, we settled into marriage and domesticity in a model similar to my parents'. I dreamed of a life happy, fulfilled, and secure.

Later that night, I found myself praying again. This time, it was *salatul istikhara*[21], the prayer

---

[21] Special prayer for guidance.

for guidance. I quietly whispered the dua, asking for direction from my creator.

Yet, even as I uttered those prayers, I knew in my heart that my fate was sealed. How could I deny Jahid? He seemed stable enough. He was seeking an education. My father liked him, and most importantly, he was a practicing Muslim. On what grounds could I say no? I knew I wasn't strong enough to face disappointing my parents. I thought of the expectations that they had for Sadiya, and the way her actions had humiliated them. All of this made me feel as if I had no other choice. I didn't want to be another source of sadness in their lives. So that night, my prayers morphed from seeking guidance and counsel to seeking comfort with my decision, and eventual happiness with Jahid.

Chapter 10

The day I laid on the cool tile floor of my bathroom, I reflected on all that had led up to that moment. Like any married couple, Jahid and I had seen some struggles, yet we had also experienced much happiness together. Yes, there had been whisperings of a greater problem, but nothing had hinted to the intensity of the pain that I felt at that moment.

My thoughts turned to the weeks just before my wedding. I had resolved myself to being with Jahid for the rest of my life. Soon, I was excited about it. I enjoyed the wedding dress shopping and sorting out the details of the ceremony with my mother. Zayna had been shocked when I first told her about my engagement, but she eventually settled into helping me plan and prepare. The ceremony we had planned was so different to the one's Zayna was used to. "Our weddings last for days," she said with a laugh. "It can be so over the top. I like what you're doing."

We would get married in the masjid, of course, with a reception following at a banquet hall. The masjid's small dining hall wouldn't be big enough to accommodate everyone. I was happy that summer. I enjoyed picking out flowers and choosing the cake flavors, securing all the big and small details that seemed so important at the time.

One day Sadiya visited the house while my parents were out. We were just a few weeks away from my wedding. She had let herself in. I was on the couch in the living room reading for my summer session class. It was a five-week American literature class needed to fulfill a requirement. The fast pace of the course made it difficult to keep up with all the reading, but I was happy that it would be over the week before the wedding.

"*Assalam Alaikum*," she said as she came over to sit next to me on the sofa.

"*Wa alaykum salam*, sis," I replied, barely looking up from my book. "Mama and Daddy are out," I had assumed she wanted to speak with one or both of them.

"Anaya," Sadiya took a deep breath. "I want to talk to you." My mother's sewing table had been pushed into the corner of the room, and my wedding dress was hanging on a hook on the wall. My mother was doing some alterations to the gown. Sadiya looked at the dress intently. "Is this really what you want?" With these words, my sister gestured towards the dress in the corner of the room.

My eyes settled on the dress as well. I knew she meant more than just the dress itself, meaning all that it represented. Her face looked tense as she stared at it.

"Sadiya, what do you mean?" I asked this question, knowing exactly what she meant.

"Anaya, don't you want to finish school, and be independent for a while before you get married? You don't have to do this you know," Sadiya's words caused me to stiffen up. Did she think I was being forced into this?

"I know I don't have to... no one is forcing me. I will finish school. Sadiya, there's nothing wrong with getting married. There's nothing wrong with following the Qur'an and sunnah," my voice raised slightly at these words. The tone of accusation wasn't intended, but it was too late to take it back. Sadiya knew what I meant.

Sadiya took a deep breath, and simply said, "Okay...I know you don't want to follow my path, and I would never suggest that you do, but I just hope you know that you don't have to get married so young to follow the Qur'an and Sunnah, and you don't have to follow everything Mama and Daddy tell you to do. Allah did give us all free will...that's all I have to say," Sadiya look at me. She had sadness in her eyes.

Free will...I thought about that. "Sadiya you're using your free will to live with Dreaux without being married. I am using mine to have a halal marriage." It was silly that she was trying to give me advice on anything.

Sadiya and I never were close, but that was the day our relationship changed forever. I knew I had hurt her, yet in my mind I was right and she was wrong. She attempted to hug me, yet I shrugged her off. She left that day hurt. I never mentioned the exchange to anyone.

All of this was swirling through my mind that day as I laid on the bathroom floor. I knew I couldn't stay there forever. I decided to get up off of the floor and shower. I turned the heat up high, but not hot enough to harm the baby. I remembered my midwife's warnings about extreme temperatures. I brushed my teeth, and applied a thick layer of coconut oil to my belly. At four months, it was only starting to protrude out slightly. Zayna had warned me about stretch marks, and advised me to use lots of natural oils to prevent them. I hadn't gotten any maternity clothes yet, so I settled on some drawstring pants and a t-shirt. I threw on an abaya that had been a little too big for me before. It was gray with navy blue stripes. It wasn't my style at all. It had been a gift from my mother, and I was thankful for it in that moment.

Looking in the mirror, I didn't appear to be pregnant at all. I hadn't gained any weight yet, and my midwife had warned me just last week about eating a little more at each meal to accommodate the growing baby within me. Thinking of this, I made myself some buttered toast and made a silent dua that my body wouldn't reject it. As I chewed carefully on the toast, and sipped on some water, I looked at the time. It was almost 1:00pm. Perfect. I would make it to the masjid just in time for dhuhr[22] prayers.

I got in the car, and drove the familiar route from my home to Masjid Al-Ihsan. My father had retired as lead imam there a few years ago, yet I still considered it another home. Imam Ibrahim, the current Imam, had studied intensively overseas, and it was his full-time job to lead the congregation, teach classes, organize retreats, and offer counsel when needed. It was counsel I sought that day, as I pulled up to the familiar building.

Walking through the door always brought a flood of memories. I longed for the simpler times of my childhood, clinging to my mother as she baked pies in the masjid kitchen which she carefully wrapped and sold on Fridays. It was almost as if I could smell the clove and cinnamon that she used. Yet I knew the kitchen was mostly empty now. My mother just didn't have the energy to bake as much as she used to. Now, her pie sales were reserved for Ramadan [23]and Eid[24].

---

[22] Midday prayer.

I climbed the familiar steps just in time for the *iqama* and offered prayer in the women's area. There were only a few sisters present, and I settled into the familiar motions of the prayer, whispering my *dua* afterwards. Just being in the peaceful calm of the masjid stilled my mind. I actually felt a sense of peace for a few moments, but soon the prayer was over, and I remembered why I was at the masjid for Dhuhr Prayer on   a   Tuesday.

I walked back down the stairs into the Masjid's foyer. I patiently waited as Imam Ibrahim greeted a few of the brothers, answering questions and sharing a few jokes. He noticed me standing off to the side and greeted me with a smile. "Sister Anaya! *Assalam Alaikum*," he looked surprised to see me here in the middle of the day, without there being an event taking place. Truth be told, my attendance in the masjid had been slacking for a long while. I had allowed the hectic pace of events in my life to inhibit me from going. While I was still an undergraduate student, attending hadn't been an issue, but once I began working on my Master's degree, and writing and presenting essays, there was always an excuse not to attend. Then there was my thesis to work on. I had still kept up my prayers, and fasted during Ramadan. I always paid my *zakat*[25]. Yet,

---

[23] Islamic month of fasting.

[24] Islamic festivals occurring twice a year.
[25] Charity.

going to the masjid had been all but abandoned. Being in that familiar space, breathing in the musky oud and praying on the rugs that had grown thin from repeated usage, made me yearn for the days when I was there on a daily basis.

Even though I rarely attended the masjid outside of Ramadan and Eid, all of the brothers knew me and I was still considered "the Imam's daughter." They parted ways as I approached Imam Ibrahim.

"I need to speak with you privately, Imam." I practically whispered. He swiftly ushered me into his office. He left the door cracked so that we wouldn't be completely alone together and sat stiffly at his desk. On the walls were paintings of Islamic calligraphy, and the desk was strewn with knick-knacks, which I imagined were from his travels and studies. I picked up a ceramic incense burner. It was inlaid with a small mosaic pattern which spelled out the name of Allah in Arabic.

"Is this from Morocco?" I asked, even though I already knew the answer. I hadn't taken the trip to Morocco while I was an undergraduate, all those years ago. Even though I had easily attained the scholarship, I allowed wedding plans to deter me. My parents and Jahid didn't want me to go, anyway. It wasn't appropriate for me to travel alone.

Yet, he promised me that he would take me the following year. That year passed and the trip never took place. After a while, I stopped asking. However, I continued to study the country, collecting many books on various topics related to the history, artwork, and culture of the region. I would often pick up the books and enjoy looking at the photos of the brick laid alleys, the mosaic tile patterns on the doors and fountains, the huge platters of couscous, and the stunning mosques. It used to bring me happiness, knowing that one day I would see all of that beauty for myself, but as the years passed and the trip never came into fruition, the thought of Morocco made me feel irritation.

"Yes," Imam Ibrahim answered. "I got while I was studying Arabic in Fez." I nodded.

"Fez is the religious capital of Morocco," I said under my breath. I had read a lot about the city with its many mosques.

"Yes. It is. I had some wonderful times there. Have you been?" Imam Ibrahim seemed more comfortable now that we were discussing something familiar.

"No. I haven't gone," I said, shaking my head. "But I've always wanted to." I looked down, wondering if I would ever get to take that trip.

"Do I need to pull Jahid's coattails? Ya'll should definitely go before things get busy with the baby," Imam Ibrahim said with a laugh. I looked up sharply, wondering how he knew about the baby.

"I'm sorry if I offended you," he said. "Your father told me about you expecting. I pray Allah blesses your pregnancy and the birth." He went on to say a few words in Arabic. I suddenly felt dizzy. I took a few deep breaths hoping not to become sick in the Imam's office. "You know my son, Khalil, might be going there to study Arabic in a few months. My wife and I might be staying there for a few weeks to get him settled in. Maybe you two should join us," the Imam looked at me intently waiting for a response.

"Are you ok?" he asked finally. "Should I get you some water?" He looked concerned.

I shook my head. No. I wasn't okay and water wouldn't help things. At this point, I wasn't sure what would. I took in a deep inhalation, mentally counted to seven, and exhaled slowly. I had been listening to a CD on dealing with stress during my commute to work, and it had advised this method. I did this a few more times, and soon my heart rate slowed to a normal pace, and I was able to speak.

"Several months ago, Jahid started acting strangely," I said. I took some more deep breaths and slowly began to recount all that had happened the past year. "Jahid has never been super attentive to me, but something just seemed off." I thought about the many nights he would be ostensibly working, and if I complained about his long hours away from home or tucked away in the home office, he would say I was ungrateful, and should appreciate all he was doing to provide for us.

"I mean when we first got married, we would take time to go for walks or to the movies, but once he started working, he became more and more distant. But we would usually make time on weekends to go to the bookstore or coffee shop. We both usually have a lot of work, but we always tried to spend a few hours in the same space." I thought about the many afternoons we spent chatting about work and school. Jahid used to listen to my essays when I was an undergraduate. Even though he quit school and started working soon after we got married, he would critique my essays, and as I struggled through math classes, he was happy to help.

"This can happen a lot between couples. It's easy to grow apart if you don't share similar interests," the Imam said. "My wife and I make it a point to read the same books, and take trips together. If we don't, it becomes difficult to forge a connection," he finished. He thought our problems were simply growing apart. I had to make it clear that it was so much more than that.

"That's true. Jahid and I tried that for a while. If we read a book together it becomes a competition on who can read it faster or gain a better understanding," my thoughts turned to how he would lecture me on the content of the Islamic books we tried reading, and if I disagreed with his point of view, it would become a bone of contention for weeks afterwards. "Once, I got my undergraduate degree and started working on my Master's he tried to go back to school and suddenly stopped. He wouldn't tell me why. Then I found out he had failed his classes. I tried to talk to him about it, but he refused. Since then he refused to read my essays. He hasn't read my thesis either. It's become harder for us to connect even more since I've been teaching."

"Well perhaps it was a blow to his ego or sense of self to have failed in school," the Imam replied.

"I know it was," I said with a nod. "However, I feel like a couple should be able to communicate and share their lives. When I talk about my job or writings, he shuts me down." I wondered why I was going on this tangent. Yes, all of this hurt, but it wasn't the real reason for me being in the masjid on that day.

"At the beginning of this year, a friend of Jahid's called him. His wife needed a job and Jahid's company was hiring," I sighed. I felt sick, but I knew I had to continue. "So, she started working there. At first, I didn't think anything of it. In fact, I was happy that Jahid was able to help out another Muslim couple. They have two young children and I know they needed the extra income, but soon Jahid's behavior changed even more. Everything I did became wrong. Even the way I dress or that fact that I don't wear much makeup...he even stopped coming to bed." I felt even more sickened thinking about the many nights, I had slept alone, while Jahid was in his home office, his face aglow in front of his computer monitors. When he did come to bed, our love making felt rushed, and rough. Gone were the days when we cuddled afterwards. He would quickly shower and return to his "work." Or when he did sleep beside me, he kept his back to me making me feel unwanted.

"I asked him over and over, so many times what was wrong. He denied anything was. He even went so far as to say it was all in my head. When we found out I was expecting, Jahid was so happy. But then things started getting even worse." I thought about Jahid's huge smile when I showed him the positive pregnancy tests, and the tender way he had placed his hand upon my tummy silently making dua for the unborn baby. Then I thought about the last two prenatal visits he had missed, saying he had to work.

"I think you and Jahid just need to reconnect, Anaya," Imam Ibrahim said with a sigh. "Jahid is probably working more now, because he feels extra pressure. The coming of a baby can put a lot of stress on a young man. He might not know how to deal with it. That might cause him to retreat and pull away from you."

"That's what I assumed at first, too.... then I found this," with this I opened my purse and pulled out an email I had printed just a few days ago. I had taken pains to white-out the name of the sender, but the recipient was Jahid. I thought about my own reaction when I had first read it. The waves of hot and then cold that had washed over my body. The way I had vomited everything that was in my stomach and the sweat and tears that followed. I handed the papers to Imam Ibrahim and watched as he read the emails.

The Imam's face looked horrified. "Who sent this?!" he asked. I confirmed that it was Jahid's friend's wife. The one whom he had assisted in securing a job months ago. I gave her the respect of not mentioning her name, even though her words showed how little respect she held for herself, her marriage, or mine.

I had read and re-read that email so many times since finding it. I couldn't remove the words from my mind if I wanted to. Even now, there was an ache in my heart thinking about the way she had compared Jahid to her own husband, saying he was better looking, a better provider. She wrote about how much respect she had for him. She got even more bold, saying how she couldn't wait to share her bed with him. It was when I got to this point in the letter that I would usually vomit. I had vowed never to read it again. Yet the words were imprinted in my mind, and I couldn't forget them if I tried. Her email had felt like a knife in my heart, yet his reply had hurt even more.

"How did you get this?" Imam Ibrahim asked. Maybe it was only my mind that made me feel that he was chastising me.

"It was by accident," I stated. I told him about the afternoon just two weeks ago when I had been home working on grading some papers. Jahid had come home much earlier than usual, complaining of a stomach bug.

"Now you know what I've been going through all this time," I had laughed. He didn't laugh along with me. I could see he was really nauseous.

"I really just need to lie down," he had said. Jahid did look paler than usual, and his skin felt clammy. He went upstairs that afternoon, and climbed into bed. After checking on him, I had gone to the kitchen to make him some tea. His computer bag, which held his work laptop, and his personal tablet had been left near the door, and I went to move it into the closet. As I picked it up his tablet fell out of the bag. Oddly enough it was unlocked, and I noticed his wallpaper had been changed from a photo of us to a random beach scene. Then an email from her popped up. It was a simple work request, yet the way she addressed him seemed too familiar. My soul told me something wasn't right. My curiosity got to me and I scrolled down through their communications. Eventually getting to this email and also his reply. Even though my mind was racing, I had emailed the messages to my account and erased the evidence.

I never did bring him his tea that afternoon. I left the house after reading the email and went to Zayna's house. I only told her I was feeling sick. I spent the afternoon in her son's bedroom, leaving the bed to vomit in her guest bathroom. She brought me cool towels, tea and water crackers.

"Sister Anaya, I have to admit this doesn't look good, however as Muslims, we must give each other the benefit of the doubt and The Prophet Muhammad peace and blessings be upon him said, 'Do not search the faults of believers and do not follow their faults; because he who follows his brother's faults, his own faults will be sought by Allah; and he whose faults are sought by Allah will be disgraced, even if he stays in his home.' Now I want to help this situation, but this is a one-sided email. We don't even know if your husband replied." Somehow, I felt like I was the one being judged. I did my breathing exercises for a few moments before speaking.

"Imam, he did reply and he continues to have communications with this woman." I began to remove his reply from my purse. Tears stung my eyes. Yet I didn't want to cry in front of the Imam. I tried to steady myself. I tried not to think about the fact that my husband had not only welcomed her advances but also complained about me to this woman. Had said he couldn't wait to share a bed, a home, and a life with this woman. This was a woman who I had prayed next to, who had eaten in my home, a woman who I considered my sister in faith. The ugliness of it all was too much to bear.

116

"Sister Ayana, I don't need to see that," he refused to even look at my husband's reply. "He isn't here to defend himself, and I don't feel comfortable with reading that." I was taken aback. I had come to the Imam for assistance, and he was treating me like I was the one in the wrong. "I can see that you're distraught," the Imam continued. "But please remember that even if these emails were exchanged there's no proof that anything has actually happened yet. At the end of the day you will only be held accountable for your own actions."

"Imam, I don't know what to do. I really just want Jahid out of my house." The last few weeks had been horrible. When I first presented him with the evidence, Jahid had continued to lie to my face. I thought about the way he had called me irrational and said I was accusing an innocent woman. Then he left, and didn't return for two days. I told the Imam all of this.

"Well, what happened when he came back?" Imam Ibrahim asked.

"At first he was apologetic. He admitted that he had crossed the line. He made promises to keep it professional...but he's still communicating with her." At this point I couldn't hold back the tears any longer. The Imam handed me a few tissues. I had seen them for myself. The text messages peppered with heart eye emojis. The declarations of love and affection coming from two married people. I had to guess at his phone's

117

password that time, because he began keeping his devices locked at all times. Was it wrong for me to intrude on his privacy? Yes, but in my mind, I was doing it to protect myself. I had to know what was going on for myself in the face of lies and secrecy.

"Sister, the last thing you want is for him to leave your home." I looked up at the Imam confused. "Hear me out, your husband is obviously in a weak state right now. If you put him out, you're leaving the door open for him to commit even more wrongs...you're allowing Shaytan to win." My heart started to race again. *I'm allowing Shaytan to win?? Wasn't it Jahid who opened the door in the first place??*

"You have to remind Jahid of the sweetness of a *halal* marriage. Cook for him, talk to him, make love to him. Remember that there's no proof that any of this has gone beyond talk. Try your best to offer him some calmness and serenity." Now tears were flowing freely from my eyes. They weren't tears of sadness, but an expression of anger. I felt rage for the first time in my life on that day, and not just towards Jahid, but also towards the Imam. I had come to him for help, hoping that he would offer some useful counsel or assistance, and I was now being encouraged to assist in my own oppression. The thought of making love to a man who was actively betraying me was too much. I gathered my purse, said my salams and left the masjid. For the first time in my life, I left the masjid in a worse state than I had entered it.

118

Chapter 11

I started my car and drove off with no idea where I was headed. Despite the Imam's suggestion, the thought of returning home and being a good wife to Jahid made me feel sick. Was that really what a good Muslim wife was supposed to do? What about enjoining good and forbidding evil? I wondered if Jahid had come to Imam Ibrahim with the same complaints against me, would the Imam have told him to be a good husband in the face of my deception. I had already given Jahid multiple chances to be honest and stop the inappropriate communications with her and yet they continued from both sides. The feelings of betrayal settled in the pit of my stomach. It felt like I had been made to ingest a vile, poisonous substance, and had visited the doctor only to be told to be patient and ingest more. I was struck by the unfairness of it all.

Suddenly my thoughts turned to *her* husband, Bilal. *Did he know about all of this?* At least I had the advantage of being aware of Jahid's deceit, yet there was a strong chance that her husband was unaware of his own wife's actions. In a sense, he had trusted Jahid when he reached out to him to assist his wife in securing a job. The realization that Bilal was being deceived too made my stomach turn.

I didn't know Bilal well. He was a quiet brother, always willing to volunteer in the masjid. I had often seen him carrying tables and passing out bottled water during iftars. In fact, that last time I saw him was at a community picnic. He had been chasing after his young son and daughter. When it was time for prayer, he was one of the brothers laying out white sheets to use as prayer rugs. He had always been respectful and kind to me in the past. I suddenly knew what I had to do.

I pulled over into a store parking lot, and fished in my purse for my phone. I had placed it on silent while I was in the masjid, and saw that I had missed a few calls. Two from my mother and one from Zayna. Yet I didn't dial either of them, instead I got ready to call Bilal. I had the numbers to most of the brothers in the community, from the days when I worked on multiple committees in the masjid. The phone began to ring before I could talk myself out of what I was about to do.

I heard the second ring and lost my nerve. I moved to hang up, yet his voice answered before I could end the call. *"Assalam Alaikum,"* his voice cut through the fog in my head. "How are you Sister Anaya?" It suddenly felt foolish to be making this call. My heartbeat was heavy, pounding in my ears. I considered hanging up, but I eventually managed to verbalize a greeting.

"*Wa alaikum salam*," I replied. I considered what I should say next. My thoughts were jumbled. They floated around in my head like clouds. I eventually came to the realization that Bilal was talking. He was actually in mid-sentence.

"...been meaning to call and congratulate you guys personally. I saw your father at Jummah prayer last week and he told me the good news. I pray Allah blesses your growing family. I was just telling Mina that she should reach out to you..." on he continued as my thoughts drifted. *Mina.* The mention of her name sickened me. His conversation seemed so relaxed. He really had no idea. I suddenly doubted I was strong enough to deliver this blow to him. I felt dizzy.

"Bilal, I hate to cut you off, but I have to speak with you about something..." I paused, unsure how to continue on. "Jahid and Mina...they've gotten much too familiar with each other. There have been some emails and text messages exchanged on both sides..." I couldn't find the words to describe just how inappropriately they were behaving. My heart was racing again. I worked on my deep breathing exercises. "I just think you should talk with your wife. Nothing about this is right. Nothing. I'm sorry." I hung up before Bilal could respond. I felt like I had just slammed a sledge hammer on his marriage. I knew I had no reason to feel guilty, yet I did. Unhappiness filled me and washed over me in waves. Suddenly the tears returned and with them the dry heaves. My stomach tried to empty itself, yet there was nothing in there to reject. I had never felt so helpless. This was a fight I could no longer handle on my own.

****

I awoke the next morning to the sound of Zaid's tricycle bell. The melodious ring, ring, ring, followed by his playful laughter were almost enough to make me smile. Zayna's son, Zaid was two years old. I looked around to realize I was sleeping in his room. I smiled when I realized I was covered with his Paw Patrol blanket, surrounded by his beloved stuffed animals. The bed was close to the window and the sun was shining intensely through the curtain. I pulled it back to see Zayna encouraging Zaid to push the pedals on his trike.

How long had I been asleep? I vaguely remembered driving to Zayna's house. Then it hit me. I had confessed everything to her. I had a slight recollection of the disgusted look on her face as I told her everything I had been struggling with for months now. I didn't want to think about the tears I shed the night before or the breakdown I had almost had. I was torn between relief that I had finally told someone and sadness over the fact that now my facade was gone. I could no longer pretend that everything was alright or that the situation would simply work itself out.

I wanted to get up, find my phone and begin to figure things out, but my body wouldn't allow me to move. I still felt so tired. I closed my eyes and allowed the exhaustion to win. In a moment, I was asleep again.

The next time, I awoke to Zayna's timid knock on the door. "Come in," I managed to answer. My throat was dry.

She came in carrying a tray which held a mug of chai, some toast and scrambled eggs. "I think you should try and eat something,"she said, placing the tray down on the bed. I went for the tea first, enjoying the milky sweetness. She sat on the edge of the bed with a concerned look in her eyes, as she observed me.

"What time is it?," I asked while taking a bite of toast. I was shocked that it was nearly dhuhr time. I had been sleeping for twenty hours.

123

"I tried to wake you for *Fajr*, but you were really knocked out. I got worried for a while," she said with a forced laugh.

"Zayna, I'm so sorry to impose on you like this. I just didn't want to burden my parents with all of this." I couldn't bear the thought of telling my parents everything.

"Anaya, it's no problem at all. You know I'm your guardian angel." We laughed at this. It brought back the memory of how we first met, me soaking wet in the storm and her protecting me from the flood. I thought about all that had happened since then.

Zayna had done the henna for my bridal shower. I remember her careful application of the delicate designs on my hands and feet. The thin henna tube she used was wielded as a tiny paint brush. Zayna carefully wrote our names on my skin with the henna paste, she wove them seamlessly into the paisley and floral patterns. "Now Jahid will have to find them on your wedding night," she said laughing raucously. The look on my face must have been one of shock. I remembered my mother and Sister Qadira joining in the laughter.

Zayna had gotten engaged to Rahim a year after I got married to Jahid. And while I couldn't do her henna, I held Zayna's bridal shower. My mother and I carefully baked and decorated miniature cakes for the occasion.

124

Zayna was now a member of the family, and my mother treated her as a daughter and often referred to her as "my Indian child." She meant it in an affectionate way, and Zayna never took offense to the term of endearment. We had spent so many happy times together. Yet this was by far the saddest event we had ever experienced together.

"Anaya, I spoke with your mother," Zayna said. Her words were enough to force me from the comfort of the bed. I stood abruptly, immediately feeling dizzy. She was quickly at my side, trying to help me back into bed.

"I didn't tell her anything. She's just very worried about you, since you haven't been answering your phone and neither has...Jahid." Zayna spit his name out like venom. "I told her that you weren't feeling well and came here to rest. She had a lot of questions, but I didn't know what to say." Zayna rubbed my shoulder in an effort to calm me down.

"Anaya, don't worry about that. Don't worry about anyone but you and that baby. Allah will work everything else out." I nodded. I knew in my heart that Zayna was right. My body and this baby had rights that I needed to fulfill. I forced myself to finish the tea and toast. I finally ate the eggs, which were the most substantial thing I had eaten in days. I began to feel a little better.

125

"You know Anaya, I have always been so impressed with your strength," Zayna said. I had never considered myself a strong person, yet the people around me always have. So many people saw qualities in me that I had trouble seeing within myself. "Since the day we met, you've always been a role model for me. The way you wore your *hijab* with such dignity on campus, and the way you married Jahid and didn't let it stop you from finishing school and getting your Master's...Allah has blessed you in so many ways, and it might be hard to see right now, but you will get through this. You already have such a strong *nur* inside of you, and when you get through this it will only grow stronger. You're going to shine so brightly it will almost hurt to look at you." With this Zayna gave me a long hug. I silently thanked Allah for putting her in my life.

After prayer, Zayna and I sat on her couch watching a Bollywood movie, sipping tea and snacking on cookies. Zaid ran around the living room entertaining himself with his toy trucks and cars. Rahim was at work, so I was able to relax without my hijab on. I wore some of Zayna's pyjama bottoms and a t-shirt she had lent me. The plot of the movie centered around a wedding and the many ceremonies and festivities were met with comedic situations and misunderstandings. Sitting on her couch, laughing at the overly dramatic acting in the film, I was able to forget about everything for a little while. I was thankful for the afternoon spent with the frivolity of the film.

126

Being around Zayna and Zaid nurtured something in me that I hadn't been nourished in a long time. Yet, soon the movie was over and I knew that I had to go home and face Jahid. I loved and appreciated the comfort of Zayna's home, but I knew I couldn't hide from my problems anymore.

Even though I had no idea what would happen, I got dressed, hugged Zayna and Zaid goodbye, and headed home.

Chapter 12

During the drive home, I came to the conclusion that there was only one way I would stay in my marriage. Jahid would have to promise never to speak with Mina again. We would have to enter counseling and stay in it until the baby was born and maybe even afterwards. I also thought it was a good idea for Jahid to look for a different job.

I never considered the possibility that Jahid wouldn't agree to these terms. I was carrying his child, and we had been together for nearly seven years at this point. Even through all of our problems, he had never denied that he loved me. Jahid had allowed Shaytan, The Ultimate Deceiver, causing him to lose sight of all this. Perhaps Shaytan had struck him at a moment of weakness. Despite it all, I had faith in the thought that when he was faced with the possibility of losing me, Jahid would come to his senses and agree to my terms.

Retrieving my phone from the car, I saw I had missed many calls from my mother, Jahid, and my father. There were also text messages from Jahid. "Call me now!!!" read the most recent. I immediately assumed his many text messages and calls were proof that he was concerned about me, worrying about my safety. It reminded me of an incident that had happened soon after we moved into our new home from the small apartment we had shared.

One morning, while fixing oatmeal, I saw a rat in the kitchen. I had been happy that early morning even though I was surrounded by half-way unpacked boxes and had to search among them, first for a saucepan and then for bowls and spoons. Just as I turned from the stove, I saw the fat creature. His body was pressed against the small area under the cabinet, his ropey tail curled around him. Only the small light over the sink was turned on, and his beady eyes were alit like tiny glow-in-the-dark marbles. It was before dawn. We were fasting that day, and the oatmeal was our suhur[26] meal. I had screamed and thrown a frying pan at it as I ran from the kitchen.

Jahid came running downstairs at the commotion. He wrapped me in his arms. "Don't worry, I'll take care of it," he said. I remembered his warm arms around me, his beard smelling of musk, and my faith in his promise. I knew I was being overly dramatic, but I refused to enter the kitchen until he did.

That night, he took up a post downstairs. He had placed traps all over the kitchen, and sat on the threshold of the kitchen door with a bat poised in his

---

[26] Pre-dawn meal eaten before fasting.

hand. He had stayed there in the hard kitchen chair until morning, when he could finally tell me he had been successful. "I got it! I killed that sucker. It was HUGE!!" he laughed at the time.

I suddenly realized this was the last time I had really felt protected and cared for by my husband. I also realized that this incident had occurred nearly two years ago. Wasn't a wife supposed to feel protected and loved by her husband daily? I knew something was missing in our union, but I was now determined to fight for our family as long as Jahid was willing to conquer that battle with me.

Pulling into the driveway, I saw Jahid's car. I took a few breathes. I tried to calm my mind and focus on exactly what I wanted to say to him. Entering our home, I began to remove my shoes, when I heard Jahid talking loudly on the phone.

"This isn't how we intended for all of this to happen, but it might be a good thing. Don't upset yourself, we'll figure everything out," he said. It became harder to hear as his voice lowered. I didn't want to think about who he was on the phone with. I quietly crept closer to the living room. "Baby, we'll work it all out... Don't worry about her. She will have to accept you." *Baby?* I prayed that somehow, I wasn't hearing correctly. Was he really talking to her? The thought of it conjured up an ache inside that I had never before felt. He began to whisper quietly and I could no longer hear.

130

I crossed the threshold and made my way quietly up the stairs, I could now hear his muted whisperings grow louder. "Mina, it doesn't matter...You're in *iddat*[27] now. Isn't that what you wanted?"

I felt nauseous again, realizing that he was indeed talking to that woman. My head was spinning. The words of the speech I had been practicing in the car deserted me. The strength that Zayna had helped me gain, disappeared. I felt just as weak, dizzy, and sick as I had the day I left our home. It seemed impossible that only the day before I had snatched our portrait from the wall and slammed it on the floor. It felt like a lifetime ago. Yet, I could see that our marriage was in just as bad a state as it was that morning. In fact, I couldn't see how it could get any worse.

I reached the creaky top step, when Jahid hurriedly ended the call. Entering our bedroom, I could see Jahid seated on the bed. His phone was in his hand. The room looked just as chaotic as it did that morning. In fact, our portrait was still on the floor. Upon seeing me, Jahid gave me a look of relief. He got up and rose in an attempt to embrace me, but the thought of hugging or kissing him intensified my nausea. For the first time in our nearly seven years of marriage, I pushed my husband away.

---

[27] Period before an Islamic divorce is finalized.

131

Feeling slighted, Jahid tried to compose himself. "Anaya, where have you been? Everyone has been worried about you. Your parents are concerned." His face now showed an expression approaching annoyance.

"I was at Zayna's. Have you spoken to my parents?" I remembered that Zayna had said he hadn't even answered their calls.

"Do you think it's acceptable for a Muslim woman to be away from home without even telling her husband where she's going to be? And no, I haven't spoken to your parents. I had no idea what to tell them," Jahid replied.

I couldn't believe he was using my sense of duty and responsibility against me. He knew I took my role as a wife seriously. I would always call or text message him before I left the house. If I was going to be working or studying late, I would cook his dinner ahead of time, and when I was out of town for a conference, I would cook meals that I froze for him to reheat. I believed in the Islamic role of a wife, and tried to never forget the magnitude of my responsibility nor the reward that awaited me should I fulfill it.

Many times, I had heard my father say from the pulpit, "When a woman observes the five times of prayer, fasts during Ramadan, preserves her chastity and obeys her husband, she may enter by any of the gates of Paradise she wishes." Yet, I was stunned that

Jahid would mention the Islamic commandments required of me, while he was in the midst of shirking those required of him while assisting in helping another Muslim woman do the same. I suddenly felt hot.

"So, you think it's acceptable for a Muslim man to pursue another man's wife behind her husband's back? Maybe you should tell my parents that you're in a haram relationship with a married woman." I practically spat the words out. I couldn't believe that they had come out of my mouth. I had never spoken to Jahid in such a derisive tone. Yet, I was angry. In the past, when we discussed Jahid's indiscretions, I had never spoken to him angrily. Instead, I begged for him to end it. I remember asking him tearfully, "What can I do differently? What can she offer you that I can't?"

When he said that I had made it easy for him to fall into the relationship because I hadn't made enough time for him and I didn't make a point to share any of his interest in technology, not only did had I listened to his complaints, but I took the blame. I allowed him to lay the burden of our marital problems and his sinful behavior upon my shoulders. In that moment, I realized that I had done everything a wife is supposed to do and more. Jahid and Mina were solely to blame for all of this. My anger in that moment reflected the realization that I had allowed Jahid to manipulate me for the last time.

Jahid raised his eyebrows at me. "Somehow Bilal found out about everything. He declared divorce upon her, and she's in *iddat* now. Yes, all of this never should have started, but I can't leave her to deal with all of this on her own." Jahid sat down on the edge of the bed. He covered his face with his hands and sighed. "I didn't mean for any of this to happen, but now I have to make the best of it. Anaya, I want to marry her once her *iddat* is over."

His words literally deafened me. He said more after this. I saw his lips moving, yet I couldn't hear his voice. A high-pitched squeal began to echo from my ears. For the first time in my life, I felt driven to the edge of insanity. I saw him get up, collect his keys and leave the room. I assumed he left the house as well. I had no words to speak. Yes, plural marriage was allowed in my religion. I knew that, and there were even polygynous marriages in our community. Yet, this situation, the lies, deception, and betrayal that had already taken place made the thought of that type of arrangement feel heinous. I wondered would the union even be considered lawful and permissible considering how it began.

My nausea returned full force. I ran to the bathroom with just enough time to empty the contents of my stomach into the toilet. Tears streamed down my face as the putrid acid burned my throat. I eventually

134

sat on the cold tile floor and attempted to collect myself. Shame washed over me. I felt like a shell of a woman. My whole life, I had made a point of living for the akhira[28]. After all, the hereafter was to be my ultimate resting place. A true believer should go about the Earth as if he were a traveler. Yet here I was stunned and frozen by Jahid's words and actions. How could I allow a man to bring me to this point?

The life I had so carefully arranged was falling apart around me. I was powerless to stop the downward spiral. I felt like I was drowning. It seemed that the more I fought against the current, the faster the waves pulled me under. Everything was out of my control. In truth, I had never been in control of any of it. I knew I ultimately had to submit to God's will, but what did that mean? Was I supposed to stay in a marriage with a man who had been so dishonest and deceitful? Was it the right thing to be in polygyny with Jahid and Mina? I had never wanted to share my husband, especially not with a woman capable of behavior that bordered on adultery. It seemed insane that Jahid expected that of me. Yet what was my other choice? I was pregnant with his child. The salary I received for teaching two courses at the college was barely enough to put gas in my car and pay a few bills around the house. I had never been independent. I had gone from my father's home to my husband's. I indeed

---

[28] The afterlife.

did feel like I was being pulled under by the waves of sadness, frustration, and disappointment.

I was in a half-conscious state, when I felt a force pulling me up. In my hazy recollection, I saw a figure helping me up. She appeared as an apparition. She was a silent figured swathed in white. I don't remember her lips moving. I wouldn't have been able to hear anything anyway; my ears still rang with the high-pitched noise that began when Jahid spoke those words. She gently washed my face in cool water. Then helped me to change into night clothes. I was too helpless and weak to feel any embarrassment. She helped me to make *wudhu*[29]. Finally, she laid out a few of my prayer mats and prayed with me. That night I reached a state in prayer that I had never attained before. As I pressed my forehead against the prayer rug, I felt as I was on an alternate plane. There I was able to hear again. I heard a quiet voice whispering the phrase *"tawakkul*[30]*"* over and over again. I finished my prayer, and the silent figure tucked me into bed. I could smell a fragrance akin to rose and musk as I drifted off to sleep.

---

[29] Ritual cleansing done before prayer.
[30] Trust and reliance on God.

Chapter 13

Tawakkul. I had heard the phrase so many times throughout my life. It means the ultimate reliance and trust in Allah's plan. I remember hearing my father talking about it many times on the minbar[31]. He spoke of the Prophet Muhammad's nearly perfect example of *tawakkul*. In one sermon, he spoke about how the Prophet lost so much when he began to propagate Islam. This led to being cut off by friends and even family members. In that time, he relied upon his first wife Khadija and his Uncle Abu Talib for comfort. "Our beloved Prophet had been receiving revelation for nearly ten years, when he experienced what has been come to be known as the Year of Sorrow. This period came after there had been a boycott against our Prophet's clan, these were times of hunger and starvation. In this year, our Beloved Prophet, may the peace and blessings of Allah be upon him, lost his wife of nearly twenty-five years. Just a few short months later he lost his Uncle Abu Talib."

My father went on to speak about how, without the protection of his uncle, the people of Mecca

---

[31] A short flight of steps used as a platform by a preacher in a mosque

were now openly hostile towards The Prophet. He spoke of a woman throwing sheep intestines mixed with animal dung on him while he prayed. "Our Prophet's daughter was understandably angry upon seeing this and wanted him to take revenge upon the woman, Yet Our Prophet only said, 'Be patient. Allah will protect your father.' The Prophet Muhammad, exhibited complete trust in Allah. Yes, he was human and experienced sadness, but he never allowed those feelings to overtake him. He trusted in Allah's plan." My father also spoke about how Our Beloved Prophet wasn't in sorrow that year due to the deaths of his wife and uncle. He trusted that Allah would care for their souls. "He felt sadness because during that year the propagation of Islam slowed down."

My childhood memories are filled with stories like this, detailing the strength, courage, and reliance on God that the Prophet and those around him exhibited. These stories became my model. They were the standard. I sought to uphold these examples, and when I didn't I was hard on myself. Yet, when the worst experience of my life occurred, the pain seared my heart like hot coal. I was stunned into a state of confusion, where all those stories were forgotten. Yet, that night, that whispered phrase, *tawakkul*, was enough to remove the fog that had been clouding my mind. I was reminded of the promises of God. I was reminded of a verse of Qur'an that Sister Qadira often repeated, "Indeed what is to come will be better for you than what has gone by."

That night I awoke at 3am and I prayed. In my prayer, I recited Qur'an in a way that I never had before. Even Surah Fatihah held a renewed meaning for me. My heart and soul begged for the guidance and mercy of Allah. After praying, I began to make t*hikr*[32], repeating "*hasbunAllahu wa nimawakil*[33]." I proclaimed that Allah was sufficient for me, and that only He could remedy my ills.

I was carrying a child.

My husband was in love with a married woman.

I had never supported myself before.

I had just finished a semester of teaching two introductory history courses, and had told my supervisor that I would be sitting the next semester out. I had planned to spend that time going to doctor's appointments, shopping for baby clothes, and nesting. Now, I was unsure of everything. Even if I returned to the college, my pay there was nowhere near enough to support myself. I was unsure of everything.

---

[32] Remembrance of God.
[33] Allah is Sufficient for us, and He is the Best Disposer of affairs

Yet I was sure that Allah would take care of me. Knowing that promise, my soul was able to rest that night.

****

The next morning, I awoke to the scent of my mother's cooking. At first, I thought I was dreaming, yet I could smell the rosemary that she always puts into her fried potatoes. I could hear the sounds of a lecture being played. The shaykh's voice was familiar. I had heard it many times in my parent's home. My mother would listen to the same lectures over and over again while cooking or cleaning the house. I'm certain she had many of them memorized. This particular lecture was about diseases of the heart and their remedies.

I found the energy to climb out of bed, wash my face and go downstairs. My mother wore her house *abaya* and her head was wrapped in white cloth. She was at the stove, stirring a pot of grits. She was so immersed in her work, that she didn't see me watching her at first. The stark whiteness of the fabric reminded me of the angel that visited me last night. My mother turned to grab one of the bottles of seasoning that were on the counter when she saw me. "Anaya, there you are. How are you feeling? When I came over last night you looked sick as a dog." When she came over last night? So, it was my mother who had silently helped me dress. Not an angel, but close.

"I'm feeling a little better." Actually, I was. The sight and smell of my mother's cooking made my stomach rumble. She was making eggs, seasoned potatoes, cheese grits, and beef bacon. I felt hungry for the first time in what felt like forever. My mother wore an apron which read "No pork on my fork." It made me smile. I remembered buying her the apron at a conference many months ago.

"Your father is on his way back from the masjid," my mother said. "He's meeting with Imam Ibrahim." My mother shook her head and frowned. I had a feeling that I knew exactly what the meeting was about.

"Mama, how did you know to come over here last night?"

A look of distaste came upon my mother's face. "Bilal called your father yesterday. When we first heard about this, I refused to believe it. We tried calling you

141

and Jahid and neither of you would answer. Then Imam Ibrahim called your father...Anaya, I'm so sorry." I could see tears in my mother's eyes. She dabbed at them with the edge of her apron. My mother embraced me. Wrapped in the security of my mother's embrace, I felt relaxed for the first time in months. Truly, my mother had never failed to comfort and put me at ease. I couldn't think of a time my mother had ever rejected me. I tried to find comfort in that fact. Yet, what had I done to earn Jahid's rejection? That thought filled me with mourning. As much as I tried to redirect my thoughts, I couldn't get Jahid's words from the night before out of my mind. *Anaya, I want to marry her once her iddat is over.* What had I done to deserve this misery?

As my mother finished up breakfast, I sat at the table sipping the mint tea she had poured for me. I thought about all that had occurred over the past several months. I asked myself why I hadn't reached out to my parents and let them know what Jahid was doing. Why had I chosen to keep it all to myself for so long? I came to realize that I had been ashamed to tell anyone, especially my parents. Throughout my life, my goal had been to seek the pleasure of Allah first, and my parents second. I couldn't shake the feeling that perhaps I had done something to bring all of this into fruition. Mentally, I knew I had been the best wife I could be to Jahid. I had followed everything I was taught a good Muslim woman should do and be. Yet, the feelings of shame and embarrassment permeated my psyche. My mind created all types of causes for Jahid's actions. Adding on to that, doing anything to earn the disappointment of my parents, felt unendurable. My mind was racing, and I attempted to calm myself down. I did my breathing exercises and sipped on my tea. I gripped the handle of the tea cup, as if it was the only thing keeping me grounded to reality.

Now, I knew that my parents didn't blame me, yet it felt unfair that my parents had to bear the brunt of the situation. Both my parents were getting older. I didn't want to burden them with all of this. It felt like I didn't have a choice in it, though.

My father walked into the kitchen with a booming, *"Assalam Alaikum!"* Years standing on the minbar had left my father with a voice that was akin to yelling. His voice seemed to make my tiny kitchen vibrate. He wore his usual tall white kufi and a dashiki. My father gently kissed my mother on the cheek, and sat across from me at the table. I noticed a few more gray hairs in his beard. Now, it was almost completely gray, with only a few spare black hairs remaining.

He placed his hand upon mine, and squeezed it slightly. I tried not to cry. My father didn't make eye contact with me, and in that moment, I knew that this hurt my parents nearly as much as it was hurting me. "Allah will provide," he said simply while taking in a deep breath. I knew he was trying to hold himself back from saying too much in that moment.

My mother served breakfast, bringing us plates piled high with eggs, potatoes, beef strips, grits, and biscuits. I wondered how my mother had prepared such a spread using the meager offerings of my kitchen. That was my mother though. My father made the *dua*. In his typical style, he interspersed his Arabic phrases with English ones. His words were so familiar to me.

"Ya Allah, we thank you for this food, and we ask that you bless the hands that prepared it. Ya Allah we asked that you bring peace and restore order to this home," my father said. I wondered what it would take to restore the peace and order that my father prayed for. *"Allahuma Barik lina feema razaktina, wa keena athaban nar,"* he finished with an Arabic *dua* asking Allah to bless the food and protect us from the fire.

I tried to eat, but ended up simply pushing the food around on my plate. I took a few bites of potatoes and a mouthful of eggs, washing it down with tea. My stomach lurched.

"You alright, Anaya?" My mother sat at the edge of her seat, an anxious look washed upon her face.

"I'm fine, Mama...just feeling a little sick." Suddenly, I felt hot.

My father let out a slight sigh. *"Subhan Allah*, she doesn't need to be dealing with all of this in her condition." I knew my father meant to speak his

144

lamentation under his breath, yet he was still nearly shouting. "This negro..." My father stopped when he saw the unhappy look on my mother's face.

"Let me just use the bathroom," I managed to let out. I ran upstairs and made it to the toilet just in time. I couldn't remember that last full meal I had been able to keep down. This couldn't be good for the baby.

My mother was knocking at the door. "Anaya, are you alright?"

"I'm ok," I replied. I washed my face with cool water, and opened the door. My mother immediately grabbed my wrist and felt for my pulse.

"When was the last time you used the bathroom?" she questioned. The look on her face scared me a little.

I shrugged. One day was going into another. Everything seemed hazy. I was dizzy again and sat on the closed toilet seat.

"Anaya, I'm taking you to the hospital, your heart is racing...you haven't been using the bathroom. You're dehydrated. That's dangerous for the baby and you."

The ride to the hospital was fuzzy. I do remember being hooked up to an IV for the first time in my life. The nurse on duty placed the thin needle into my arm. With her cold hands, she inserted the tube and taped it into place. The bag of saline hung from a metal rack on wheels.

The part I remember most was the ob-gyn on duty was a very slender Indian woman. She must've weighed less than a hundred pounds. She was charged with the task of wheeling in a heavy and cumbersome portable sonogram machine. I wanted to get up and help the poor woman as she attempted to twist and turn the hefty machine. My father was in the waiting room, but my mother was by my side as the doctor applied the greenish gel to my stomach. "We just want to take a look at the baby, and see how everything is progressing," she said. With that she placed the probe upon my lower abdomen, pressing the instrument into my belly. A faint picture eventually showed up on the screen. I found myself holding my breath as I saw my baby for the first time. "Ah, she looks good, and don't worry, I call them all 'she.' Too soon to tell gender just yet."

A single tear fell from my eye, as the doctor pointed out the tiny arms, legs, and finally the heartbeat. It appeared on the screen as a flickering light, faint but strong and steady. Despite all of the chaos that was happening in my life, my little bean was steadily growing and changing. It seemed miraculous — it was miraculous. In that moment I vowed to do better for that little being that was growing inside of me. It wasn't my fault what had happened up to that point, but it was my fault for allowing Jahid's actions to affect me in that way. In that moment, I said *no more*.

Chapter 14

My midwife's name was Kaye Johnston. She was a kind white woman about the age of fifty. She wore her salt and pepper hair in a short pixie cut that accentuated her deep blue eyes. Her smile was kind, her hands always warm. She was the type of person who could remain unflustered even if she were on a sinking ship. Her calmness washed over me as she pressed and palpated on my tummy. "You had a little scare, there, Anaya," she said pressing the fetal heart rate monitor to my abdomen. It was less than a week after my visit to the emergency room for dehydration. I left that day with a prescription of Zofran and orders to stay in bed and drink water, Gatorade, and soups round the clock.

Yet, when we left the hospital that day, I knew what I had to do to stop the waves of sickness that continued to wash over me. That night, I told Jahid if he wanted to continue a relationship with Mina, he could. That was between him and Allah. However, I would not be a part of it, and I could no longer be married to a man capable of such deception.

I can't go on like this," I said. "I want you to divorce me." I almost choked on the word — divorce, but I refused to cry. I refused to beg. I had done enough of that. I decided to resign myself to whatever Allah had in store for me. I committed myself to *tawakkul*.

In my heart, I wanted him to beg for me back. I wanted him to admit his mistake, and vow to walk away from her. I wanted him to choose us, our baby and the life we had created together. Yet, we plan and Allah is the best of planners...

None of that happened. He simply kissed me on my neck and muttered, "I'm sorry." Jahid looked sad, defeated, and lost. He left that day with a bag of clothing and shoes. I changed the locks on our home the next morning. I heard him try his key in the lock the next night, but I ignored it. I didn't let him in. I didn't answer the phone for him, either. He pronounced divorce upon me through text message and I had to laugh. Nearly seven years of marriage dissolved just like that.

I stopped vomiting the day I changed the locks. In that instant, I had taken my power back. I realized I had allowed it all to make me forget who I was. I tried to see myself that way that Zayna and my parents saw me. The Anaya they knew was worthy of so much more. I was worthy of so much more. I trusted that Allah had more in store for me.

Yet, as I sat in Kaye's office, a small part of me hoped that Jahid would walk through the door. He knew about my appointment that day, I had put it in our shared calendar. A part of me wished that he would walk in with a dramatic apology. That didn't happen, either.

Finally, Kaye found the right spot on my abdomen that allowed me to hear the baby's rapid heartbeat. It sounded like a fast thumping, the galloping of a horse.

"Have you been taking the Zofran?" Kay asked. She was referring to the pills they had prescribed me after my visit to the ER. I shook my head, no.

"Actually, I haven't gotten sick since that day." It was true. Perhaps it was the absence of Jahid in the house, or maybe it was my resolve to trust in Allah's plan. Either way, it was over, and for that I was thankful. That morning I had eaten a bowl of oatmeal with raisins and cinnamon. I had savored a cup of peppermint tea. It felt like a victory to be able to eat without becoming nauseated.

"Kaye, how long is it safe for me to travel?" A few nights ago, I had begun to look through my books about Morocco. The familiar images provided me with comfort, and my desire to travel there filled me with longing. I had started researching guided trips, but I hadn't mentioned it to anyone yet. I didn't have the money anyway, but the fantasy offered a welcome distraction from all that was going on.

"You're a first-time mom, and you're young and healthy. You can travel up to 35 weeks. Where are you planning to go?" Kaye looked at me carefully.

I shrugged. "I'm not sure yet, just wondering."

"Well, the best time to travel is between 18-24 weeks. That's when you'll be most comfortable. Nothing like being on a plane in the last trimester, no fun at all, trust me."

Kay began to talk about foods I should avoid, but I wasn't fully listening. I had read pages and pages on the topic from pregnancy books and magazines, and I was also doing math. I was now sixteen weeks pregnant. If I really wanted to travel, I would have to work fast. I wondered if it was even possible.

"So, where's that husband of yours? I don't think I've seen him since your first visit," Kaye's eyes seemed to interrogate me. I could tell that she knew something was off.

I took a deep breath, and tried not to show a reaction, but still the tears materialized out of nowhere. It had been like this for me the past few days. One moment, I would feel fine, even strong. I would be cleaning or organizing something in the house, and suddenly the sadness would wash over me. The tears would fall. I would make *dua* or say my *thikr* until the

150

feelings would fade. Yet, I wondered how long this would last. I hated feeling unbalanced and unsure of my emotions. This was honestly the first time in my life that I felt out of control. Yet, I began to realize, I had never truly been in control.

Kaye handed me a tissue, and patted my back. It was odd, but I allowed myself to be comforted by her. "Whatever it is, remember it will all be alright in the end, and if it's not alright, it's not the end." Her words resonated with me. The truth of them struck me to my core.

"Kaye, I honestly don't know where he is...I don't really want to know," I said. She looked at me with kindness in her eyes. "It's all kind of complicated."

"Honey, it always is," she sighed. "Just allow yourself to feel what you're feeling, and treat yourself with patience and kindness. Focus on you and that baby," she said as she patted my tummy, which was just beginning to show a small bump. "It may work out with him, it may not. You can't control others, you can only control your thoughts, feelings and reactions. I wish someone had told me this a long time ago." I listened to Kaye's words. She was right, I couldn't control him. I was only just beginning to gain control of my own thoughts and emotions. Yet, each day I was learning to be more patient with the situation and with myself. Each night, I was calling out to Allah in prayer and *thikr*. I could feel myself changing.

151

Chapter 15

That afternoon, I found myself seated across from Suhaila Hassan. I remembered Suhaila from our days growing up in the masjid. She was just a few years older than me. Over the years we had lost touch. Yet, I could see that she was thriving. I remembered one of the last times I saw her was the very first time I met Jahid, and it seemed ironic that now I was in her law office asking about how to go about seeking a divorce. Her office was small, but well furnished. Her waiting area had two brown leather sofas adorned with brass thumbtacks. There were a few large framed paintings of floral scenes.

In her office, Suhaila had her degrees proudly framed. Her pre-law degree from Dillard was alongside her Juris Doctorate from Tulane. I found myself in awe. I was proud of what she had managed to accomplish. I hoped I would be able to hold it together in front of her, yet I reminded myself that if I did break down, that was alright, too. On Suhaila's desk was a framed photo of her and her husband, Rasheed. They were flanked on the left and right by her two children, a boy and a girl, wearing matching outfits. Her husband and son wore crisp white shirts, while Suhaila and her daughter wore white dresses. Her daughter had a huge white bow in her hair and she was missing a few teeth, adding to her adorableness.

Suhaila had her curly hair pinned back into a low bun. After hugging me, she got down to business. "So, would you mind giving me a little background? Why do you want to file for divorce?" When I had originally called Suhaila on the phone, I had been pretty vague. I only said that I no longer wanted to be married and Jahid felt the same.

"Well, Jahid is in a relationship with another woman." I stated this matter-of-factly, just as I had practiced in the car. With these words, Suhaila looked down. She got up from behind desk and gave me a hug. I wondered how many more people would be giving me concerned hugs before this was all over. I didn't like people feeling sorry for me. I wasn't used to the recipient of sympathy.

"You know, I heard that there's a pregnant sister in the community whose husband basically abandoned her..." Suhaila didn't make eye contact as she continued. "Were they talking about you, Anaya?"

Abandoned? That word felt so harsh, yet what other word was there? Jahid hadn't considered me or the fact that I was carrying his child when he gathered his clothes and left. His text messages didn't express any desire to reconcile either. He nastily accused me of putting him out of his home, yet he was the one who

153

had left after refusing to end things with Mina. He hadn't put any money in our account since he left, and he hadn't asked how I was, or how I would pay for the midwife visits. One of his last text messages had stated, "You're trying to make me out to be the bad guy. You're the one who changed the locks on MY HOUSE!" It hurt that he could be so heartless, yet nothing he did lately surprised me.

I nodded. It hurt that my story was already becoming the subject of gossip, yet I couldn't really be shocked. Our community was so small. My story was bound to have made the rounds by now. Suhaila patted my back, "I'm so sorry, Anaya. I promise, I'll help you in any way I can." Suhaila seemed to be almost near tears herself, yet she quickly pulled herself together.

Suhaila returned to her desk and began taking notes on a yellow pad. She started with simple questions, like when had we gotten married, had we always lived in Louisiana, and who had paid the bills throughout our marriage. "Some of the questions will be getting a little personal," she said timidly. "Just answer as best you can. When was the last time you were intimate with your husband?"

My face burned with embarrassment. "Is this really necessary?"

"Anaya, in order to file for divorce, you have to be living in a *bona fide state of separation*. If you're still being intimate, then that wouldn't be the case."

I thought for a moment. Could I even remember the last time we had been intimate together? The last five months seemed to have been filled with nothing but arguments, and when we weren't arguing, we were ignoring each other. Yet, the day I found out I was pregnant, Jahid had actually been happy. I remembered him smiling so wide that his dimples showed. "Say *wallahi!*" he had demanded while laughing. I showed him the positive pregnancy test as proof.

That night, we went out to dinner. It had felt like a fresh start. I thought maybe he would stop finding fault with everything I did. Maybe he would start paying more attention to me than he did to his phone, tablet, and laptop. Yes. That was the last time we had made love, nearly three months ago. In the months leading up to that, he had been more and more rough and rushed in bed. Yet, that time, he had actually been caring and taken his time with me. I took a few deep breaths. Her simple question had stirred up so many emotions. It was like a pendulum swinging from the intense joy upon finding out about the baby to the depression of losing Jahid. That was the last time he had touched me lovingly, and he likely never would again. Then there was the intense anger at him and Mina for putting me through this.

"Are you ok?" Suhaila looked concerned.

"I'm fine...It was three months ago," I said calmly. Suhaila continued to jot notes on her pad.

"Anaya, would you like to use adultery as your grounds for divorce?" Suhaila had that concerned look in her eyes again. "If you have proof that he maintained a relationship with her, then it would be in your best interest. If you file with divorce as your grounds, you'll be more likely to receive alimony, and other assets. I mean, don't you want to be able to keep the house and your car?"

I mulled this over for a moment. The thought of putting adultery on the divorce papers seemed fair. Our marriage hadn't simply dissolved on its own. Mina had cruelly begun to tear our relationship apart the day she sent that first email. Truly, they both deserved to be outed, and the thought of doing so gave me a twisted sense of vengeance, but I shook my head. "Can I get those things without accusing him of adultery?" I couldn't see myself making that type of accusation. While I had seen the text messages and emails that had gone back and forth between Jahid and Mina, there was no clear proof that they had been intimate with each other, and I refused to play dirty.

"It's possible. We can file for a no-fault divorce, and see how it goes. Jahid might agree to alimony during mediation, or it could go before the judge. We'll just have to stay patient and prayerful and see how it all plays out." Patient. That word had been coming up a lot lately.

"Now there's one more issue we have to discuss," Suhaila said looking down. She took a deep breath before continuing on. "You know, Anaya, divorce can truly bring out the worst in people. Especially in a situation like this, when one party is clearly wrong, it's not uncommon for the guilty party to throw around accusations of wrongdoing on the innocent party. Now, it's best to be prepared and not be caught blind sighted. Is there anything that Jahid could bring up in court against you?"

"*Against me?* There's nothing he could say against me unless it's an outright lie!" I was raising me voice. Suhaila's words had angered me. In my marriage, I hadn't been perfect, but I had never done anything against Jahid. Certainly nothing that was close to what he had done — was doing to me.

"Well, consider what he has been doing up to this point?" Suhaila was right. Jahid had been telling lie upon lie. It hurt to think how my loyalty had been met with deception. "I know it hurts, Anaya, but we have to be prepared. Is there anything he could say against you in court?"

I thought about all the excuses Jahid had made in the last few months to justify his behavior. According to him, I hadn't been affectionate enough. I spent too much time worried about my education and my writing, and I didn't really listen to him. "It's all about you. It always has been," he had hurled at me harshly. *He had said that.* I didn't respect him as a woman should respect a man. I had never been a good wife. "No other man will ever put up with a woman like you who cares more about her studies than her husband's happiness," Jahid spat these words out just a few days before I had finally walked into Imam Ibrahim's office. This final indictment against me had hurt more than all the others.

"Well, Jahid started insulting me towards the end of our marriage. He began to complain about things he never mentioned before. He called me selfish, said I wasn't a good wife..." It hurt to admit these things to Suhaila.

"Well, it's typical for a man who has been caught red-handed to try and hurl insults. I hope you didn't take any of that personally. I pray he doesn't try and come up with anything else. If you think of anything, be sure to let me know."

Suhaila asked a few more questions, and had me sign paperwork. With that and an agreement to pay a $2500 retainer plus $250 an hour, the process of my divorce began. I had no idea how I would get the money. What I had in my savings account was running out quickly, and Jahid hadn't given me anything since leaving days ago. I realized that the state of my finances was another thing I would have to be patient with. I left

158

Suhaila's office with a packet of paperwork to look over and the relief of setting things in motion. I tried not to let the stress of it all get to me. I began to *thikr* as I drove home, *hasbanullahi wa ni'ma wakeel.* I prayed that Allah would help resolve everything in the best way.

***

A few days after my visit with Suhaila, I sat on a cushion on the floor of Imam Ibrahim's sitting room. Embroidered cushions and Persian rugs were laid atop the hardwood floors. There was a thin cloud of bakhoor[34] scented smoke in the room. It wafted through the air like a woody scented fog. The walls were adorned with portraits of Arabic calligraphy. Just as in his office, there were knick knacks from his travels scattered

---

[34] Incense.

about. A wooden camel sat on a low coffee table next to a few egg shaped paperweights made from natural stones. There were a few bookshelves as well, filled with texts in Arabic and English.

Sister Nabila, the Imam's wife, had welcomed us with hugs and offers of tea or water, which we all refused. They had a two or three-year-old daughter named Aisha. She had stared at us with her large brown eyes, when we first arrived. She clung close to her mother's side, hiding her face behind the ends of Sister Nabila's long dress. Their teenage son, Khalil, greeted us with *salams*, and then retreated to a room in the back of the house.

To my right was my mother, who rubbed the back of my hand periodically. I could see that she wanted to be brave for me, yet she looked just as upset as I felt. When she thought I wasn't looking, she dabbed at her eyes with a tissue that she kept in her sleeve. She would sigh occasionally, and couldn't seem to keep still. Yet, she refused the chair that the Imam's wife had offered. To my left was Zayna. She had a dark green scarf draped over her dark hair and wore a black abaya devoid of decoration. In her hands were wooden beads with which she used to perform *thikr*. Her husband was watching Zaid so she could be present. This was the longest I had seen her go without talking. She sat solemnly on her cushion, whispering her *thikr* quietly.

On the opposite side of the room was my father. He had his arms folded stiffly and hardly made conversation with Imam Ibrahim who sat on his right. The Imam nervously made small talk and offered us cookies that were arranged on a tray. My father had invited Jahid's father, yet he had refused to come, saying, "I don't want to get involved at this point." Words were exchanged, but I hadn't been made privy to everything that was said.

We heard the ding-dong of the bell, and I could feel the tension in the room increase as Imam Ibrahim went to answer it. Was it him? I heard my sister's voice greeting the Imam and apologizing for her lateness. I wasn't expecting Sadiya to be here today. My sister had her head wrapped in a green and gold African print fabric. She wore wide-legged black pants and a long sleeved tee shirt. She gave salams to everyone, and hugged mommy and Zayna before giving me an extra long embrace. The relationship between my sister and I had become somewhat strained over the years. I didn't think it was intentional on either of our parts. Our lives had become so different, that it had become hard to connect. It felt good to have her present though, surrounded by her, mommy, and Zayna I felt protected. I felt safe.

The bell rang again, and I braced myself. I knew this time, it had to be him. Imam Ibrahim rose again to answer it. *"Assalam Alaikum."* I heard Jahid's voice. I could feel the energy in the room shift as we all heard a female voice coming from the foyer. *It was her.* I had come to terms with Jahid's disrespectful behavior, but no one in the room thought he would have the gall to bring her here. Still, she entered the room with Jahid and Imam Ibrahim.

"This fool done lost his mind," Sadiya's words were barely under her breath. Yet they expressed what everyone in the room was thinking. I was barely conscious of the fact that I was rising to leave.

"I can't do this," I said as I prepared to leave. Zayna, Mommy, and Sadiya were at my side immediately, helping me back to my cushion. I wanted to shove them all away, but I didn't want to make a scene.

"Anaya, be strong. We have to face this sooner or later," my mother said. I tried to steady myself. Why would either of them think it was appropriate for her to be here? I felt like I was trapped in a nightmare. How much more of this craziness was I supposed to endure? I didn't want to see either one of them. I had allowed myself to be talked into the meeting mostly by my father and Imam Ibrahim. I didn't think there was any hope for my marriage, but Imam Ibrahim had stated, "If there really is no hope for your marriage, the least we can do is allow it to end in a way that pleases Allah. I won't feel at peace, or like I've done my duty if I don't at least try to address this situation. Let's not forget that there is a child involved."

I had allowed myself to be talked into this meeting, but I only agreed to it if my family could be there. And yes, my family was there, but so was she. Nausea washed over me again, but I refused to allow them to see me hurt or angered. I returned to my cushion as calmly as I could. My mother was right, I had to face this sooner or later.

I looked at my father, whose face expressed what everyone in the room was thinking. He held a sneer mixed of disdain and disgust. I knew he wouldn't be able to hold his tongue for long. Jahid took his seat a few feet from my father. I refused to look at Mina, but I could see her out of the corner of my eye. With downcast eyes, she hesitated before moving to the corner of the room. There were no more cushions available, so she sat on a rug near the wall.

Imam Ibrahim began to make dua. "*Bismillah*[35]. Oh Allah forgive all our sins, the minor of them and the major of them, the first of them and the last of them, the ones committed secretly and openly. Oh Allah, I ask of Your pleasure and for Paradise, and I seek refuge from Your displeasure and from the Hellfire," he said. We all finished with a collective "*Ameen*[36]."

"I called this meeting because as you all know, our Ummah is like one person. As our beloved Prophet said, 'The parable of the believers in their affection,

---

[35] In the name of Allah.
[36] Amen.

mercy, and compassion for each other is that of a body. When any limb aches, the whole body reacts with sleeplessness and fever.' And by Allah, you can ask my wife, I haven't been able to get a restful sleep since I learned of all of this," Imam Ibrahim took a pause as he rubbed his beard. He seemed to be searching for the right words. I doubted he had ever been in a situation like this.

My father used this as an opportunity to interject, "I gave my you my daughter. I entrusted you with her, and this is what you do *akh*[37]? I accepted you as a son. Gave you a seat at the head of my table! This is the way you repay us?" my father was almost yelling. He could barely control himself. The anger and pain in his voice was impossible not to hear.

"Listen, I didn't come here to be yelled at," Jahid replied. There was a bit of contempt in his voice. I looked at him for the first time since the day he gathered his clothes and left. He wore a navy-blue *thoub*[38] that I had given him. His beard, which he normally kept trimmed was unkempt.

"Let's all calm down. I know emotions are high, but let's not allow them to get the best of us. Now, Jahid, I have to advise you, as your brother in Islam, that your actions are bordering on *haram*. This is all so

---

[37] Brother.
[38] Men's garment.

164

ugly. We have to come up with a plan to rectify it," Imam Ibrahim tried to gain control of the situation.

"There's nothing to rectify, Imam. Anaya asked me for a divorce, and I granted her one. Since then, she hasn't even let me in my own house." Jahid's attitude was without remorse. In fact, he seemed to be angry with me. I began to wonder what kind of man I had really married. "I only came to this meeting out of respect for you, Imam. Me and Anaya have gone back and forth about all of this for months. Mina is going to be my wife soon enough, and if Anaya can't accept that, then so be it."

"You can't make intention on another man's wife! What kind of Islam are you practicing? This whole mess is *HARAM* and you can't make the *haram, halal*. Period," my father was standing up now and moved towards Jahid. Imam Ibrahim positioned himself between them. I looked at my mother, my sister, and Zayna. They all looked just as shocked and awed as I felt.

Imam Ibrahim attempted to calm the two men down. "Jahid, do you think that a relationship that starts with *haram* will end in happiness? Sister Mina, do you think Allah will bless a union that started based on the pain and misery of another woman? And you're still married to your husband."

Mina began to speak up, "Brother, I'm in *iddat* and—"

"Imam, Anaya made a choice," Jahid cut off Mina. "I asked her if she could accept Mina as a co-wife once her *iddat* is over, and she refused. No. Everything didn't start in the right way, but we're making it right the best way we can," Jahid replied.

"This is sick and twisted," my mother blurted out. "Don't try to blame this on my daughter."

"Jahid, you can't make intentions upon a married woman. That puts any marriage between you two in danger of being invalid. Islamically and legally you're still married to Anaya. She is still your wife. Are you going to provide for her and your unborn child? She tells me that you haven't given her anything since you left," the imam was still attempting to iron things out peacefully. My father and Jahid had returned to their seats, yet they both glared at each other. I had to commend the imam for continuing to reason with Jahid. It was clear to me that he was going to handle things the way he wanted regardless of what anyone said.

"She put me out of my house. I have to find a place to live and provide for myself. She put herself in this position, when she asked for a divorce," Jahid's words were cold.

The room sat in silence for a moment. Everyone was at a loss for words. I don't think anyone thought that Jahid would be this callous. He seemed to be a completely different person from the man I married. I began to wonder which was the real Jahid.

166

Jahid used this opportunity to prepare to leave. As he got up and walked towards the door without so much as a *salam*, Mina followed behind him without looking back.

Chapter 16

When Jahid and I had been married for a few years, my mother got very sick. She spent much of that time resting in bed, wincing in pain. The pain emanated from her abdomen. She was nauseous constantly. After having many tests done, we discovered that she had gallstones and would have to have her gallbladder removed. My mother would never admit it, but I knew she was scared. "It's all under the *qadr*[39] of Allah," she would say. I knew she was nervous about going under anesthesia for the first time in her life. The night before her surgery, we all met at my parents' house. The intent was to send her into surgery surrounded by *dua*.

Sadiya came with Dreaux. She actually wore a black scarf and abaya. Dreaux sat off to the side. I could tell he was ill at ease in the environment surrounded by Muslims. Sister Qadira and a few of my mother's longtime friends were also there. We refused to let my mother into the kitchen. Sister Qadira, Sadiya, and I took over. Frying fish, stirring red beans, and stuffing peppers, we prepared some of my mother's favorite dishes, following her recipes to a T. We hoped her

---

[39] Will.

stomach pain would subside for a little while so that she could enjoy the dishes.

That night, Jahid had led us in a recitation of Qur'an. Reading from Surah Rahman, his recitation was so melodic and soothing that it brought my mother to tears. The words that made up the refrain of the surah, "*Fabi-ayyi ala-i rabbikuma tukathiban,*" meaning "Which of the favors of your lord will you deny?" reverberated throughout the room like the strength of a drum's beat. It touched each of our hearts. Afterwards, my father led us in a powerful *dua*, seeking thanks, forgiveness and protection for my mother.

When my mother was released from the surgery early the next morning, she told me that Jahid's recitation echoed in her mind as the drugs that would render her unconscious took effect

"The nurse told me to count down from twenty to zero, but I didn't, I recited Surah Rahman. Just the way Jahid recited it, and I knew that Allah would make everything alright."

A few days after our meeting at Imam Ibrahim's home, I thought about that night. How could the man who had given my mother that beautiful gift also be capable of such deception and underhandedness? How could the man who I had shared my life, home, thoughts, and bed with for so long have shunned me so brutally? Something was off. It was almost as if he had multiple personalities. I may

169

not have been the perfect wife, yet I knew I deserved much, much better than this. As hard as I tried to avoid thinking about the situation I was in, thoughts of it would return and consume me.

My stomach was beginning to protrude more each day. Sadiya had given me some shea butter to apply to it, even so, I saw a few squiggly lines on each side of my stomach. I knew they were the beginning of stretch marks. There were so many questions that floated through my mind. Not just those about Jahid. I asked myself how Mina could be so cold to another Muslim sister. Then, I wondered what man would ever want me again. I would be thirty in just a few years. I would be a single mother. What man would want to pick up what Jahid had forsaken? Would any man be able to accept me— nearly thirty, a single mom, with stretch marks and an imperfect body?

I knew that if I continued to ask these questions that honestly had no answers, I would drive myself crazy. It was during these times, that I would take out my *misbaha* and sit in *thikr*. My favorite, *"Hasbanullahi wa ni'ma wakeel,"* became my lifeline and protection.

One day, I sat down to read, attempting to keep my mind off of Jahid. The book, a history about the Silk Road, failed to keep my interest. Suddenly, I heard the familiar ding, of a text message coming through. I expected to see a message from my mother, Zayna, or my sister. They had all been making sure to keep in contact with me, checking on me almost every day. When I looked at my phone, it was an unfamiliar number on the screen. *"Assalam Alaikum* sis,"* the message began. "My name is Soraya, and I once attended your father's masjid. Not sure if you remember me. I was wondering if we could meet up while I'm in town?"

I tried to jog my memory for someone named Soraya, but I couldn't think of one. Our community was so small, I had to have made contact with her at some point if she had ever attended our masjid. Then, I remembered her. Soraya was a kind woman with a warm smile. I remembered her and her many children attended several *iftar* dinners and gatherings years ago. She had four daughters and two sons. Looking back, I could recall her calmly keeping the children on task, deftly managing them without ever looking overwhelmed. I hadn't seen Soraya in ages. It seemed as if she had just vanished. I wondered where she had moved to, and how she had gotten my number. I decided to text her back. I had nothing else to do that day, and maybe meeting with her might help distract me from my negative thoughts.

Soraya and I met at a small coffee shop on South Carrollton. When I walked in, I scanned the cafe and found Soraya sitting in a corner of the room, sipping on a glass of water. I walked up to her and she greeted me warmly, *"Assalam Alaikum,* sis!" She gave me a warm embrace. "Let me order you something, Soraya. What do you want?"

We approached the counter. I ordered a citrus tea with honey and Soraya got a chai. "Sister, can we take our drinks to the courtyard outback? I want to be able to speak freely," she said. I agreed, the atmosphere in the cafe was pretty hushed. There wa some soft jazz playing and people were mostly studying or engaged in quiet conversation. Once we entered the courtyard, and sat at the wrought iron tables and chairs, Soraya reached her hand across the table and grabbed my hand. She squeezed my hand slightly, took a sip of her chai and began.

"Sister, I remember you very well. When I lived here in New Orleans, you and your mom were always so kind to me and the kids. Sis Malikah welcomed me so warmly when I first arrived here from New Jersey," Soraya seemed to have such fond memories of me and my mother. I wished that I had more than vague memories of her. What I mostly remembered was how young Soraya had seemed, and how she handled so many children at such a young age. I recalled her grace and beauty.

"So, tell me, how have the children been?" I asked.

"Girl, they are getting big! Can you believe I have a teenager now?" No. I couldn't believe it. Soraya looked barely out of the teens herself. "I had another

172

son, too! His name is Zubair. We are still back up in New Jersey," Soraya continued. "I'm here for a few days visiting my aunt."

"Sister, I heard about what happened to you and that's why I wanted to reach out. Something similar happened to me," Soraya continued. I found it hard to believe that anything similar to what had happened to me had ever happened to Soraya. She was gorgeous and graceful. She looked at me intently with her honey colored eyes, and went on.

"Two years ago, this was about three years after we returned to New Jersey, I got pregnant with my youngest. Something wasn't right my entire pregnancy. Things just weren't the same between us. Whenever I approached Ayyub, he denied everything. It got to the point where he made me think I was crazy. It was ridiculous how easily he lied to me. It didn't matter that I was the mother of his children. He would look me right in the face and lie." This all sounded so familiar. Hadn't Jahid denied everything for months? My heart began to race. I didn't want to hear that Ayyub had hurt Soraya the way that Jahid continued to hurt me. Yet Soraya's story went on.

"What hurt the most was that she was someone I knew," Soraya said. How could this have happened to another sister? "Now she wasn't married. Yet, the way things went down was in no way Islamically appropriate. They got married at midnight in an

173

Imam's basement, while I was in the hospital recovering from childbirth! I have never been so hurt in my life." I could see the pain in her eyes as she described everything. Unspilled tears sat in the corners of her eyes.

"What Imam would marry them like that?" I asked. This was not the Islam I knew. Where was the consideration for the Soraya and her beautiful children?

"When I approached the Imam, he said there was nothing *haram* about the union. He said there was no reason not to marry them. The day I was set to be released from the hospital, I waited for Ayyub to pick us up. My sister was watching the rest of the children. Well, he never showed up. I had to take an Uber home with my newborn baby. He never told me himself what he had done. I heard about it from sisters in the community in New Jersey." I couldn't believe what I was hearing. I pictured her still bleeding from childbirth, coming home to six other children, and finding out that her husband had just taken another wife without even thinking to inform her. My heart ached for her.

"Since the imam said there was nothing Islamically wrong with their marriage, I tried to do the right thing. I tried to be a good co-wife, but my emotions were everywhere. I needed help with the new baby, and the other kids, but Ayyub would be gone for days at a time. He said to me once, 'You have to remember I am a newlywed.' I couldn't believe he could be so heartless."

The cruelty that Ayyub had shown Soraya struck me to my core. How were these men so capable of hurting their women without remorse? This didn't reflect the Islam that was taught to me growing up. This didn't reflect that loving and caring relationship of my parents or of other couples in the community whom I had grown up observing over the years. Where was the disconnect? What made men like Ayyub and Jahid so cold?

"Sister, I was truly a mess during that time. *Subhan Allah*...I'm a convert. Ayyub's actions made me question everything...I had never in my life doubted my deen[40]. I am ashamed to say that I allowed a man to push me to that point. My faith is stronger than ever now. *Alhamdulillah*, I didn't allow him to take that from me." Soraya stopped to take a sip of her tea.

"Soraya, how did you hold on to everything? How did you keep the faith?" I sat in awe of Soraya. She didn't look like a woman who had gone through all of that. I wondered was she now a single mother, or had she been able to hold on to her marriage.

"I turned to Allah! I released everything and completely submitted. I realized that I had to be

---

[40] Religion

good with my relationship with Allah and my relationship with myself. All of that is more important than any man on this planet. Yet, I asked Allah to help me understand how a man like Ayyub can hurt others without regret. It led me to learn about narcissism."

Narcissism? I had heard the term a few times in one of my undergraduate psychology classes. I thought back to Narcissus, the son of a God in Greek mythology who fell in love with his own reflection to that point that he died staring at it. How did this term describe men like Ayyub and Jahid?

Soraya must have seen the confusion upon my face, as she said, "It confused me too at first. I never would have described Ayyub as narcissistic. Yet the more I learned about it, the more I realized what drives men like him and how he was able to hurt me like that. Narcissists have no empathy. They are unable to see the hurt that they cause us."

I was silent as I tried to absorb all that Soraya was saying. I never considered narcissism. I honestly didn't know much about it. As I sat contemplating her words, Soraya continued on.

"Ayyub made excuses for his behavior constantly. In his mind, he wouldn't have *had* to take another wife, if I had only done this or that differently. He complained about me constantly. I tried to be patient. I thought that's what I was supposed to do," Soraya looked to be on the verge of tears. I moved my chair closer to her, and rubbed her shoulder. I was at a loss for words. I didn't want to imagine the hell she had to endure. How did she keep her head held high through all of that?

"When I thought the situation would improve, things started to turn worse. Ayyub got to the point where he barely supported me or the children. He spent all of his money on his new wife. I couldn't work with the baby being so young, and my other children needing me at home. One day, I went to the masjid to ask for assistance. They gave me some money to buy food and clothing for the kids...but Ayyub found out. That's when things turned bad," Soraya paused there. I saw a single tear escape from her eye. I handed her a napkin, which she used to dab at her eye.

Soraya reached into her purse and took out her phone. I sat confused as she pulled up a photo. "I keep this photo on my phone at all times. When I feel weak or like I would be better off with him, I look at it. One day, I'll show it to my younger daughters. My oldest doesn't need to see it. She found me on the floor that night," with these words Soraya handed me her phone.

On the screen was a picture of her, yet she was barely recognizable. Both of her honey colored eyes were swollen shut. Her lips were puffy and a sickening shade of bluish-purple. Her front tooth was chipped. There was a huge open wound on her forehead.

"Wallahi[41], I thought he was going to kill me that night," Soraya stated. Looking at the pictures of her face, I didn't want to imagine what state her body had been in after being attacked like that.

"But Soraya, Ayyub is so big...how could he?" Ayyub was a tall man, who was broad shouldered. Soraya was less barely over five feet and slight. I shook my head. *How could he?*

"Men like Ayyub are dangerous. It was looking back that I realized all the kindness he had shown me or anyone in the community, that wasn't the real him. He wanted to be seen as the perfect Muslim man, but his heart is dark. Men like him don't do anything purely for the pleasure of Allah. Men like him seek praise. I had seen this side of him in the past, but it was so well hidden. I thought to myself, no one's perfect. I wanted to keep our family together, so I made excuses for him. He had pushed me in the past and grabbed me in heat of an argument here and there, but I always blamed myself. I thought I shouldn't have raised my voice or I shouldn't have started the argument in the first place. He had only hit me one other time before that night. He had promised me he would never put his hands on me again," here Soraya stopped. She sipped on her tea and stared off into the distance.

---

[41] I swear to God.

178

"We don't have to keep talking about all this," I said to Soraya. "I see it's upsetting you."

Soraya shook her head. A look of determination returned to her face. "No sister, I'm sharing this with you because my spirit is telling me that you need to hear it. There's a reason I'm here in New Orleans right now. Allah wanted us to connect," Soraya seemed sure of this. It was amazing that Soraya happened to be in the city right now, with a story connected so similarly to mine.

"Right before I got pregnant with Zubair, I had decided to go back to school online, I wanted to earn a medical coding certificate. I was also homeschooling Zara and Yunus. I was busy. I didn't have the time to stroke his ego. Many evenings he would complain about my lack of attention. I didn't realize it, but all of this hurt his ego...it literally made him snap. I truly believe that in my heart. You see men like him have to seek that admiration and attention somehow, that's why he married her."

I mulled over Soraya's words. Jahid loved to be correct and throughout our marriage he would needle me until I agreed with him. I always had to concede to him and compliment him in order to keep peace in our home. I had thought that's just how some men are, yet maybe there was something more to it than that.

"I'm sorry for everything you've been through, Soraya." Here I paused. I wanted to ask about her relationship with Ayyub. I hoped that she wasn't still with him. I eventually was able to speak the words, "Can I ask, are you still with him?" I made a silent *dua* that her answer would be no.

Soraya shook her head forcefully. "The night I woke up in the hospital, I had no memory of how I had gotten there, but I did remember the way he hit me over and over again, and the way I begged him to stop. It was like he couldn't stop. At that point I realized how dangerous Ayyub is. He wears a mask. That's what makes men like him so dangerous. When they are challenged, and others start to see what they're really like, they completely lose control. When others in the community knew that he wasn't providing for us, the way he was supposed to, that's what made him attack me," Soraya stopped and sipped her tea.

I had exposed Jahid, but he wasn't capable of the type of violence that Ayyub was. Or was he? I thought of the photo Soraya had shown me, suddenly I felt so vulnerable. Not only was I alone, I was also pregnant. That left me in a defenseless position. However, Jahid had never put his hands on me. His words had always been enough to cut me like a knife. Still, Soraya's photo and her words clung to me, and I doubted that they would ever leave my mind.

"I'm so sorry, Anaya. I don't want to scare you. I'm sure that Jahid won't try anything with you. He hasn't ever put his hands on you, has he?" Soraya looked at me with concern in her eyes.

I shook my head. "No. He never has."

"*Alhumdullilah.* You know when I left Ayyub, he slandered me in the community. He couldn't manipulate me anymore and so he wanted to control how people viewed my character. According to him, I had a problem with polygamy, and that's what caused all our problems. And a lot of people in our community believed him, but I continue to hold my head up high. I will never let him or anyone else control me again," Soraya took a deep breath and leaned over to embrace me.

"Anaya, I'm proud of you for leaving and standing up for yourself," she continued. "I know I didn't have the courage to leave Ayyub when I was your age. Sister, don't fear for your future, Allah will bless you with much more than you ever imagined."

I allowed Soraya's words to settle over me. I prayed that she was right. Feelings of gratitude overwhelmed me. It seemed divinely orchestrated that Soraya had reached out to me on that day. It gave me a certain sense of peace, knowing that she had gone through all of that, and she was still standing strong. I had tears in my eyes, as I squeaked out a humble, "Thank you."

181

Chapter 17

I pulled and tugged at my top, trying to get it to cover my tummy. Choosing my outfit has never been an ordeal for me, but that day I had put on and taken off several possibilities. Pressed for time, I knew I had to hurry. I had written down the court date in my planner last week, and I had only an hour to get there. Yet each top I had put on sat uncomfortably on my tummy, the fabric stretched thin.

Suhaila had called me excitedly, a week prior, "I got us a court date!" she had announced. We both thought it would take months to go before the judge. Suhaila had originally said she had no idea when we would get my case tried. Somehow, Suhaila had managed to get an emergency hearing "due to extenuating circumstances."

"Now this is only a temporary hearing," she warned. "You can't get your divorce finalized while you're expecting, but insha Allah, I'm hopeful that the judge will grant you temporary alimony."

Since that day, I had been anxious about what exactly would happen in court. Even though Suhaila had assured me that the judge would be more than sympathetic to my situation, I was nervous about what types of accusations Jahid might hurl at me. He had told Suhaila that his reason for refusing to support me in any way was because I had put myself in the situation I was in. "He blames you for everything." she stated matter-of-factly. "He said if you hadn't changed the locks on the house and filed for divorce, none of this would have happened."

I wondered how he could blame me, when his actions had started our marriage on a downward spiral, and he had pronounced divorce upon me before I ever filed. I mentioned this to Suhaila, and she had no explanation to offer me. I had no idea what he was capable of at this point, and even the thought of being in the same room with him made me feel a sickening mixture of hatred, anger, sadness, and pain.

I had chosen a navy-blue pair of maternity pants which I had bought recently along with a pair of elastic-waist jeans. I purchased them the day I realized none of my regular pants could button. I had chosen a few maternity tops, that I ended up putting back. I didn't have enough money on my debit card to cover the cost.

I had planned on wearing one of the looser blouses in my closet, but then tried on three, and each one had been constricting on my growing belly. I finally found a blue and white polka dot top that had once been way too big for me. I pulled it over my head and was relieved to see that it fit. I chose a blue *hijab* and pinned it in place. I tried to find something I liked about my appearance, even though it was a struggle.

I was now gaining weight steadily, and as happy as Kaye had been at my previous appointment, I was having a hard time adjusting to the new form that stared back at me in the mirror. I was glad that my baby was growing and getting stronger each day, yet the roundness in my midsection did little to increase my self-esteem. It had already taken the biggest hit of my life. Even though everyone around me assured me that there was nothing lacking in me, it was hard to escape the thought that there must be something wrong with me. If there wasn't, why would Jahid choose another woman over me?

I often looked at other women who sat in the Kaye's waiting room, many with their partners. I could feel and see the love between those couples. The men would occasionally sneak in a belly rub, the women feigning annoyance. I imagined the men would offer assurances to their wives that not only were they beautiful in spite of their growing bodies, but they were even more beautiful *because* of the roundness of their bellies and the heaviness of their breasts. I didn't have that. My growing belly was a reminder of the blessing of the baby within me, but it was also a reminder of the relationship that had dissolved before my eyes, and the pain of all that was still so fresh that at times it took my breath away.

I had to be strong. Having a breakdown at that moment wasn't an option. If things went well at the hearing today, I would no longer have to pretend that the stacks of bills piling up on the side table next to the door didn't exist. If the judge offered me temporary alimony, then I could stop calling the mortgage company and asking for yet another extension. That wouldn't take all of my worries away, but it would remove a lot of them.

I had kept in contact with Soraya, and she had gotten into the habit of sending me encouraging text messages almost daily. I had spoken to her a day prior, trying to make sense of Jahid placing the blame on me for the failure of our marriage, "Sis, you have to understand the pathology of men like this. Some of them think it's their right to have multiple wives, by hook or by crook. You stood up for yourself and this is your punishment. It's sick, but that's the truth."

I told her I was going to court today, and she had sent me a *dua* to recite. "My sister, say this *dua* today...trust in Allah: O Allah you are my strength and You are my support. For Your sake I go forth, and for Your sake I advance, and for Your sake I fight." I said this *dua* as I finished getting dressed. I reminded myself to trust in Allah.

My first stop was my parents' home. The plan was to pick them up and drive together to the courthouse downtown. I drove down Elysian Fields. It was a cool March morning. The air was crisp, and I used the opportunity to open my window. Breathing in the crisp air of the tree lined street, I remembered driving as a passenger on the bus on my way to UNO so many years ago. My mind wandered to the simple days of being a student. My greatest worry was my grades and assignments. I sighed with the thought that I hadn't realized how lucky I had been. I turned onto Gentilly Boulevard and soon pulled in front of my parents' home. My mother was already outside. She was using the hose to water her plants: roses, hibiscus, and tulip bulbs. None were blooming yet, but within a month her yard would come alive.

My mother wore a simple black dress. Her scarf was a somber gray. Upon seeing me, she wrapped up the hose and walked over to the car. "Your father's not coming," my mother announced upon entering the car. The tone in her voice told me I better not ask why.

We drove on in silence. As I merged onto I-10, I saw my mother pulled her *thikr* beads out of her purse. She then began whispering *"subhan Allah"* quietly, as she used her right thumb to guide the beads gently over her hand, a movement I had seen her perform more and more lately. I felt a pang of guilt. I knew that this whole ordeal was putting a lot of stress on my parents. I had assured my mother that she didn't have to come, but she insisted. "I want to be in the courtroom to see how it goes down for myself. I hope the judge sees right through his foolishness, *subhan Allah*."

Soon we were downtown. I could see the superdome in the distance as I exited the highway. The sun reflected off the silver walls of the dome. I eased the car onto Loyola Avenue. I hadn't been to the courthouse in years. I couldn't help but find the dreary, utilitarian gray concrete covering most of the building odious. Suhaila waited on the steps outside of the building. In her arms was a thick binder labeled "Abdul-Aziz V. Ahmed." She had her thick curly hair pulled back into a low bun, and she wore a brown pants suit and sand colored heels. She looked ready for business, quickly exchanging *salams*, and ushering us into the building.

Once inside we had to go through metal detectors and have our purses searched. The security guards barked orders, "All cell phones and laptops must be removed from bags! No belts allowed through the metal detectors!" Suhaila seemed unbothered, hurriedly removing her cell phone and laptop from her bag, and putting them in a round dish like the ones in the airport. My mother and I followed her lead. The courthouse was overcrowded. Many people were rudely jostling and rushing others. This was a place where everyone had their mind on their own problems, and it showed in the worried looks on people's faces. Suhaila then lead us to our courtroom which was on the sixth floor of the building. The placard on the door read: **Courtroom 6A Judge Hill**."

Suhaila had warned me that many cases would be tried by the same judge that day, and that it was possible we would have to wait hours for our case to come before the judge. So, I wasn't surprised to find the courtroom crowded. We found seats near the back of the room. "I need to ask the calendar clerk a question," Suhaila said as she rushed off to the front of the courtroom.

"Well it seems like she's got everything under control, *alhumdullilah*," my mother said as she got comfortable in her seat. I looked at the time: 9:20. Court was supposed to begin in ten minutes. I couldn't help but scan the room for Jahid. In the back of my mind, I wondered if he would have the nerve to show up with *her*. As outrageous as that sounded, I couldn't put anything past him at this point.

Suhaila was at the front of the room, talking in hushed tones to a petite black woman. The woman had a clipboard in her hand which she flipped through as they spoke. Soon, Suhaila rushed back and sat next to us on the stiff wooden bench. "I have some good news, only two cases are before yours. *Alhumdullilah* your last name starts with A," she said with a smile. Looking around the packed room, I *was* thankful my name started with A. The room was close to reaching its capacity, and it looked like nearly all of the seats were gone. Soon people would have to stand near the rear wall close to the doors.

"Is it always so packed in here?" my mother asked, as she glanced around the room.

"Last year it wasn't, but our parish lost a judge, so Judge Hill is having to alternate between family court cases and criminal cases each month. It's been crazy since then. In fact, I'm shocked we got on the calendar so soon. I've been seeing family court cases drag out for months. Although, I have been basically harassing the calendar clerk lately," Suhaila answered.

Her calmness was beginning to rub off on me. She had been through many divorce cases before. She knew how the process worked, and that gave me peace of mind. Even the fact that we were in court that day was a blessing. I didn't have the option of waiting months. By then my house would certainly be in foreclosure. I said a silent prayer of thanks and asked Allah to strengthen me for whatever I was going to face that day.

A husky white man walked to the front of the courtroom. He wore a khaki colored uniform and a black tie. "You're in courtroom 6A. The honorable Judge Linda Hill will be entering the courtroom momentarily. For any cases requiring minors to testify, the minor witnesses must remain outside of the courtroom until their case comes before the judge. All cell phones must be turned completely off. Failure to do so can result in being held in contempt of court. There is absolutely no eating or drinking allowed in the courtroom. Keep all talking to a minimum. There is absolutely no audio or video recording allowed. Failure to follow any of these orders can result in being held in contempt of court." The bailiff delivered these orders in a monotone fashion. A few children were ushered out of the courtroom, by a second bailiff. They were led to a waiting room adjacent to the courtroom. This opened up some seats and those who were standing against the back wall were now able to take seats on the stiff benches. As I looked around, I spotted Jahid. He was seated against the back wall of the crowded room next to a middle-aged white woman. I wondered if that was his lawyer.

"All rise. Court is now in session, the Honorable Judge Linda Hill presiding," the bailiff announced. Everyone stood as the judge walked in. She was an older black woman with friendly eyes. She wore her light brown hair in a bob cut and small pearl earrings were her only jewelry. We were told to sit down after the judge took her seat.

"This is just like Judge Mathis," my mother whispered to herself.

"Bailiff Jones, please present today's docket."

190

"Would all respective parties and their counsel, please rise when your case is called. Abadie Versus Drew. Abbott Versus Abbott. Abdul-Aziz Versus Ahmed."

Here I stood along with my lawyer. I saw Jahid stand with the woman whom I assumed was his lawyer. She had a face full of pasty makeup, wore heavy eyeliner and dark red lipstick. I wonder where he had found her.

"The Bailiff continued to call cases, and I said silent thanks again. There were so many cases I wondered how they could possibly all be tried today. However, I quickly learned that trial was a loose term. The first case, Abadie V. Drew took less than twenty minutes. The mother had brought in the father over his share of a $257 medical bill for their son. The father agreed to pay his portion and the case was quickly resolved.

The case involving Abbott Versus Abbott was more involved. The bailiff called the case and a tall Caucasian woman stood. "May it please the court and Honorable Judge Hill, my name is Ms. Edwards, counsel for Ms. Abbott in the above titled action. We are here to determine negligence on the part of Mr. Abbott concerning the parties' minor child Quentin Abbott," the lawyer wore a black skirt suit and black pumps. Her dark hair was pulled back into a low ponytail. Ms. Abbot was a heavyset woman, she had smooth chocolate skin, and looked down throughout the entire trial. Mr. Abbott was also heavyset and tall. He was light skinned with freckles speckled across his nose and cheeks. He wore an unbuttoned tan sport coat. He kept shifting around in his seat during the trial. Mr. Abbot's deep sighs and eye rolls made it clear how he felt about being in court that day.

Throughout the trial we learned that Mr. and Ms. Abbott had been divorced for five years at that point. The shared a son, Quentin, who was twelve. Ms. Abbott complained that Quentin came home from his father's home hungry, thirsty, and wearing the same clothing in which she had sent him. "He don't even see to it that Q bathes. He wears the same dirty clothes all weekend, and comes back musty," the mother complained. The father silently objected to the mother's testimony with loud exhalations. He sat sternly with his hands folded across his chest as she gave her side of the story.

When it was his turn to speak, Mr. Abbott denied ever neglecting the boy. "Quentin eats plenty with me, your honor. I ain't starving my son. He takes a bath and dirties himself up again in ten minutes. He's a boy."

It was hard to tell who was telling the truth. Even though Quentin was one of the minors that had been sent out of the room before court began, the Judge didn't allow him to testify. After hearing from Mr. and Ms. Abbott, the judge stated, "I don't feel that it's necessary to subject the young man to testifying in a case like this. I'm appointing *guardian ad litem* to the case. The guardian will be interviewing and visiting all parties involved. The case will be revisited in three months. We will have the calendar clerk schedule you in the docket over the summer," with that the case was dismissed until a later date.

The entire case seemed odd to me. The former couple had been divorced for five years at that point. It seemed sad that they hadn't gotten to the point where they could be at peace with each other. Their body language showed the animosity that they still held towards each other. As the case was tried, I couldn't help but think about the negative effect all of that must have had on their son over the years. Then I thought about the baby that I was carrying. Would Jahid and I be able to put our feelings aside and raise our child peacefully? Suddenly it felt like my battle was only just beginning.

The bailiff called out, "All parties in the case Abdul-Aziz Versus Ahmed please step forward." My mother squeezed my hand as I left her side. There were two tables at the front of the courtroom. Suhaila and I moved to the front of the room, and stood at the table that had just been vacated by Ms. Abbott. Jahid and his lawyer sat on the other table. We were told to raise our hands, and be sworn in. We were then allowed to take our seats. "Ok, we have Mrs. Abdul-Aziz here, and you're being represented by Ms. Hassan, correct?" the judge asked.

I cleared my throat before managing to squeak out, "Yes. Yes, Your Honor."

"Alright, and Mr. Ahmed...I seem to be missing some of your information. Who is representing you today?"

Jahid's lawyer stood up, "Your Honor, I'm Maiya Sokoloff. I'm here representing Mr. Ahmed." I could now see Ahmed's lawyer more closely. She wore pinkish eyeshadow and her thick black eyeliner made her eyes look beady. The thick foundation that she wore settled into the lines around her eyes and mouth. "I'm asking that this case be dismissed without prejudice until a later date. I haven't had time to gather evidence, Your Honor?"

My heart began to race even faster. I could feel my palms becoming sweaty. If the case was dismissed, I knew it would be months until I would be seen in court.

"Well, why haven't you had time to gather evidence Ms. Sokoloff? I can see that the case was originally filed in January," Judge Hill flipped through the stack of paperwork on her desk. She seemed to be looking for a reason why the case should be dismissed. The confused look on her face showed that she was coming up empty.

"Your honor," Ms. Sokoloff began, "I have only been retained to this case last week."

The judge looked annoyed. "I can't dismiss the case based on your client's lack of preparation. Now, this is only a temporary hearing, and looking through the facts of the case that were presented to me, I'm confused as to why all of this couldn't have been settled through mediation."

Here Suhaila stood, "Your honor, may I interject?"

Judge Hill nodded, "Yes, please do."

"Your Honor, I have been attempting to come to a temporary agreement with Mr. Ahmed for the past two months, and he has refused to come to an agreement. He has also refused to meet with the court's mediation team," Suhaila spoke clearly and sharply. "During this time, my client, who is five months pregnant at this time, has been left without any means of support from Mr. Ahmed. It is my hope that we can leave court today with an order for temporary alimony of some sort."

The judge sat back in her chair. She was silent for a moment. She seemed to be at a loss for words. She shook her head before speaking. "I have read over the case carefully, and it seems as though Ms. Abdul-Aziz asked Mr. Ahmed to leave the marital home in January, and that's when Mr. Ahmed halted his support. Now, it wasn't stated in the clearly why was Mr. Ahmed asked to leave," Judge Hill looked in my direction. She obviously expected a response from me. I

195

felt frozen in place. I didn't want to say why I had asked Jahid to leave. The room was still crowded with people waiting on later cases, and I had already told Suhaila that I didn't want to bring up all of that.

"It's been my experience that when a woman puts a man out of the house there is some reason for it, especially when she is in your condition," Judge Hill was addressing me directly.

I cleared my throat, "Your honor, Jah...Mr. Ahmed has been in some type of relationship with another woman...It's been going on for many months now." The judge listened intently and scribbled some notes on her pad.

"Mr. Ahmed is this true?" She looked at Jahid, intently, waiting for a response.

Jahid said nothing. He looked indignantly at Judge Hill. "Your Honor, I don't see what that has to do with this case. She put me out of my home, and now she expects me to support her," Jahid's words sounded bitter. The way he referred to me as "she," shook me to my core "I can't support her and myself."

"Mr. Ahmed, I need to remind you that you're in a court of law," Judge Hill's eyes bored into Jahid. She seemed to be getting on her bad side, "We have a certain precedent governing cases like this. Looking at your financial information you can support her and yourself, now Ms. Abdul-Aziz has been a good wife to you for years now, correct?"

"She's been... alright," Jahid said coldly.

The judge stared down at Jahid warily, "When did you realize she was just alright? Before or after she refused to continue cohabitating with you?" Here the Judge's voice rose for the first time. She was silent for a moment. She seemed to be trying to collect herself. "Mr. Ahmed, not only is Ms. Abdul-Aziz still your legal wife, she's also carrying you child, or do you also object to that?" Jahid sat silently. I wondered when Jahid's lawyer was going to say something. "Now, according to the discovery submitted, you've been the primary breadwinner throughout your marriage, and that doesn't stop now. You've been negligent and I'm surprised that Ms. Hassan hasn't sought remuneration for abandonment as well," here Judge Hill looked towards Suhaila's direction.

"Your Honor, may I?" Suhaila spoke. The judge nodded. "Yes, that option was presented to my client and she refused. Ms. Abdul-Aziz really only wants to be taken care of in the manner in which she is accustomed. She has been struggling for several months now without any financial support coming in. It has caused an unfair amount of stress upon her and her unborn child," I could hear Jahid's disdainful snort at Suhaila's words.

"Do you have a problem, Mr. Ahmed?" Judge Hill asked. The bailiff walked lazily towards Jahid's table. He whispered something to him.

"Our court has received all of the financial requests from the plaintiff's side, we have yet to receive anything from the defendant," the Judge looked at Ms. Sokoloff.

"Yes, your honor, as I said, with me having only recently been retained, I haven't had the opportunity to put together that information. I understand that Ms. Abdul-Aziz deserves financial support, as does her unborn child, however Mr. Ahmed also needs to be able to support himself, as well," Ms. Sokoloff stated.

"Ms. Sokoloff, where is your client currently residing?" The Judge asked.

Ms. Sokoloff looked at Jahid. "I'm renting a house uptown," Jahid said.

Suhaila spoke up, "Your Honor, could you ask Mr. Ahmed who he is currently living with? I feel that this information is important to the case."

"I agree. Mr. Ahmed, who are you currently living with? You're a man living alone. You could've gotten a studio or a room for rent," the Judge stated.

Jahid shifted in his seat. Looking down, he finally stated. "I'm living with a friend and her children."

My heart dropped. How could he be living with her already? I tried to calm myself using my breathing exercises. Yet, suddenly a calmness washed over me. It was the same warm feeling that I had felt the night before. *Trust in Allah.* I sat back and simply watched everything unfold.

"Mr. Ahmed, are you to tell me that you feel it appropriate to support *a friend and her children*, while your own unborn child receives no support from you? This family you helped to create comes first," the Judge looked at Jahid with disgust.

"Well your Honor, I am allowed to take another wife in my religion, and she put me out. Why should I pay for a home that I can't live in?"

"Mr. Ahmed, she put you out rather than live with a man who has broken marital vows. I'm surprised all she did was put you out. Your religion may say you can take another wife, but aren't you supposed to support both? Are you telling me that your religion allows you to abandon one wife for another?"

Jahid and his lawyer sat in silence. "Ms. Hassan, our court received the affidavit containing the financial requests made by your client, and they seem more than reasonable. We are granting that Mr. Ahmed is to maintain the marital home, including all bills incurred for the maintenance of the home. We will also grant that Ms. Abdul-Aziz be granted $800 a month to cover any other necessities needed for her maintenance. Additionally, since your appearance here could have been avoided had Mr. Ahmed agreed to mediation, I am requiring him to pay any and all legal fees incurred thus far. Clerk, please prepare the order," with that Judge Hill let her gavel down with a bang.

I sat stunned for a moment, not realizing that the bailiff was already calling the next case. Suhaila had to help me to my feet, and usher me to the back of the room. As I got up, I felt many eyes on me. One woman seated towards the front of the room nodded in my direction and silently pumped her fist in the air. "Stay strong," she mouthed. In that moment, I realized that I would stay strong. I was done being weak. It was time for me to realize my strength. Allah was on my side. I needed only to trust in Him.

Chapter 18

I had been carrying the weight of fear and worry around with me for weeks, and in an instant the judge's gavel lifted that weight. Even though I knew that things weren't completely settled between Jahid and I, I felt at ease knowing that at least I didn't have to worry about maintaining myself or my home. I could put all of those worries out of my mind until after the baby was born. I had been trembling as I sat in my chair at the front of the courtroom, yet as the trial concluded, I felt my old determination return.

As we stepped outside of the courthouse, I hugged Suhaila, tears of relief filling my eyes. "Thank you for standing up for me," I said. I couldn't remember the last time I had felt more grateful to a person.

Suhaila had brushed off my thank you's. "Anaya, you were only asking for what was rightfully yours. The judge was on your side, as she should've been. I'm just thankful that I was able to help you." She squeezed my hand. "I pray that things will start looking up after this. You deserve some peace in your life."

Suhaila reminded me that we would have to return to court in several months to receive a final judgement. "The judge was so empathetic to you today, that I'm sure you will get everything you ask for when this is all said and done," Suhaila said.

Throughout the drive home my mother exhaled repeatedly, stating, "*Alhumdullilah*, I'm so glad that's over." My mother had been carrying a hidden weight as well. Some of the guilt I felt about the stress this entire situation was putting on my family began to lift as well. As I dropped her off to rest, she confided in me. "Anaya, you father didn't want to be here today, because he didn't feel like he could control himself in there."

"Control himself?"

"Yes...just the mention of that man's name gets your father's blood pressure up. He didn't know what he might do if he had to see his smug face today...and your father feels guilty about all of this." I wondered how my father could be feeling guilty about Jahid's actions.

"Anaya, your father gave you in marriage to that man. He feels like maybe he made a mistake allowing you to marry him." I cringed at the term, *allowing*. Lately, my thoughts had often turned to how my marriage to Jahid had been orchestrated. It was true that my parents had supported and encouraged the union, however I had agreed to it. I had walked into it with open eyes, hoping and praying that it would be best for me. How could my father, or anyone else, have

202

foreseen the ills that seemed to reside in Jahid's heart? The truth was, at the end of it, all we could do was trust in Allah's plan.

As I dropped my mother off, my father sat in the living room, anticipating our arrival. My mother recounted the events that had happened in the courtroom. "He was actually bold enough to bring Islam into it! I just couldn't believe it." My father shook his head and laughed after hearing the Judge's response. It had been months since I heard my father laugh. As I left that afternoon, my father walked me to my car.

"Anaya, I know this has been painful for you, and in part I blame myself...I swear to Allah if I could take all of your pain away, I would. I know you don't deserve any of this, but we plan and Allah plans...I pray that brighter days are ahead of you. Now, we can just focus on you and that baby," with these words he tapped my tummy and gave his *salam*.

I called Soraya that afternoon. She could barely get her greeting out before I was recounting my victory in court. "Masha Allah, wow! The judge saw right through him...Allah is so merciful," Soraya said. Yet later in the conversation her tone changed, "Is anyone staying with you tonight?" I thought about her question. She sounded worried. My mind flashed to the photo Soraya had showed me of her black eyes and bruises on her face.

"No. I think I'll be ok." Soraya was silent on the other end of the line.

"Just, please, be careful sis. Men like Jahid and Ayyub hate to lose," she warned. "Make sure you lock your door...just be vigilant, please." I felt she was worried unnecessarily, yet before ending the call, I promised to keep my guard up. After speaking with her, I said the same *dua* of protection that I had made before court.

That night, I had pulled out my laptop and searched nursery themes. I sat on my bed at ease, sipping on tea and looking at swatches of toxin-free paints. I had scrolled through nursery photos, and felt at peace with things. For the first time in months, I was hopeful for my future.

As I drifted off to sleep I remembered Soraya's warnings to me. Her words about staying vigilant, and that men like Jahid and Ayyub hated to lose, echoed in my mind. Despite myself, my dreams that night were filled with the image of Soraya's bruised and battered face. The image of her distorted face flashed in my mind, along with the look of anger on Jahid's face as the judge banged her gavel. Suddenly, I heard Jahid's voice. I wasn't sure if I was asleep or awake when I heard the banging. "How dare you keep me out of my house. And you got that *kuffar* judge to agree with you!!!" I had never heard him so angry in my life. His voice was filled with rage. Suddenly I sat up, realizing that I was no longer sleeping and all of that noise was coming from just outside of my front door.

I sat confused in my bed for several moments. I tried to make sense of the sound of Jahid's fury. His voice boomed. I could hear loud bangs at the door. I later learned that Jahid was using his feet to try and kick the door in, and when that didn't work he used his shoulder to charge against the door. My heartbeat thundered in my ears. I had brushed off Soraya's warnings, and in that moment, I felt foolish. I suddenly didn't feel so strong. I rubbed my hand protectively over my stomach. What did he plan to do once he got through the door? The image of Soraya's bruised and battered face filled my mind. Fear took hold of me, leaving me paralyzed. I heard the distinct sound of glass breaking. I realized that he had used something to break one of the two thin rectangular windows that flanked my front door.

My heart raced. I searched my bedside table for my phone. I wasn't sure if I should call the police or my parents. I unlocked the phone, and began to dial 911. Before the call could connect, I could see the red and blue flash of police lights outside my window.

Jahid's loud yells were then replaced with the stern commands of a police officer. "Hands up!! Keep your hands where I can see them!!"

"Officer this is my house! Why am I being arrested?!"

"You aren't being arrested. You're being restrained! Get on your knees! Hands behind your head!"

It all of a sudden occurred to me that Jahid was a black man in a volatile situation with police. My mind was racing with all that could go wrong. As much animosity as I had towards Jahid, I didn't want things to go they had for so many black males in similar circumstances. I was too scared to leave my bedroom. I parted the blinds to see what was happening.

Outside my window, I could see more police lights. The words of the officers became muffled. I never thought I would ever pray for Jahid again, but I suddenly found myself making dua for him. Truthfully, he had no business outside my house on that night, and he had allowed his own anger to put himself in that situation, yet I prayed that he wouldn't pay for this mistake with his life.

"Police! Open up!" The stern command was accompanied by loud raps on my door. I haphazardly wrapped my scarf over my hair and came downstairs.

I side stepped shards of glass, as I opened the door cautiously. "Ma'am do you know this man?" The officer asked. He used a bright flashlight to illuminate Jahid's face. He sat on the curb, his hands cuffed behind his back. The man whom I had once held in such high regard now looked pitiable. He hung his head low. His white t-shirt was smeared with drops of blood. I considered his question. I doubted that I knew him. Yet, despite myself, I nodded.

Chapter 19

In Sister Qadira's classes, we memorized many short surahs of Qur'an. She would recite each ayah, and we would diligently repeat after her, word-for-word. Often, she had to stop in order to correct our pronunciation, instructing us to hold certain vowels longer or place emphasis on certain consonants. She would later test us on our recitation and understanding of each surah. We would all have to pass before moving on to the next surah. This proved frustrating at times, because it was typical for some girls to hold the entire class back. Yet, this was the way she had been taught during her studies in Egypt, and she was dead set on never deviating from the way her teachers had taught her.

One of the last surahs I ever learned from Sister Qadira was Surah Al-Inshirah, meaning "The Solace." I can vividly remember Sister Qadira's strict instructions, "Ladies, the *sād* is a heavy letter...There is a *shaddah* on the *lām*... you must double it," her directions were stern, but delivered with concern. My favorite lines of the surah were *"Fa inna ma'al usri yusra/Inna ma'al 'usri yusra."* I guess because Sister Qadira often emphasized them. "Allah is promising the believer that in every difficulty there is ease. He repeats it twice in the surah," she always said.

"With every difficulty there is ease"... I had never truly had a need to truly ponder upon the wonder of these words until the year of my divorce. However, looking back, I can testify that Allah never breaks his promise, ever. Truly with every difficulty that I faced that year, Allah brought me relief in one way or another. In the end, Allah held me up and fortified me in such a way that I feel repentant that I didn't always trust in his divine plan fully.

The night that Jahid tried to break into my home, my neighbors happened to be sitting on their back deck. They had just finished having the deck put in. The older couple, who would have normally been asleep, were sitting on it and admiring the craftsmanship that the workers had done. I don't want to think about what might have happened had they not been out there and heard the noise. I try not to think about it. When my thoughts turn to that night, I use my energy to give thanks instead.

There is so much to give thanks for. Due to the attempted break-in, I was granted a protective order against Jahid. He was no longer allowed to come near me or my home. The judge ordered it to stay in place until three months after the baby was born. We would then have to go to court to have it evaluated.

With everything that was happening, Imam Ibrahim offered to act as my protector until things could settle down. He apologized for not doing so earlier. "Sister Anaya, I should have listened more intently to your complaints about Jahid. This situation has taught me a lot," Imam Ibrahim was reticent and apologetic. Now he, and the rest of the community, rallied to make things right.

I didn't want to return to my parent's home, yet I knew my parents would feel more comfortable having someone in place that I could call should I need something. I also decided that I would stay in my home until a month before my due date, and then I would live with my parents until after the birth of the baby.

For a few weeks, I didn't hear from Imam Ibrahim much. Things were peaceful, and I was finally able to begin nesting. I spent many afternoons with Zayna. It seemed I had found the ease after every difficulty. My mother would often stop by with food, and Kaye was happy to see me steadily gaining weight. The baby was growing and thriving in my belly. The baby had no idea of the chaos that it had been protected from.

Imam Ibrahim's son was to begin his Arabic language studies in Fez. Imam Ibrahim, his wife, and daughter were flying there with him in order to get him settled in the home of his host family. I knew of this, and assumed I would rely on my parents, my sister, and Zayna until he returned. I hadn't really had to depend on him for much, but it was nice to know that he was available. He would often call to check on me and would stop by occasionally with his wife in order to see about me. Imam Ibrahim called me one morning and after giving salams simply said, "We got your ticket to Morocco. The whole family is coming, and as I'm your protector, sister, that includes you!"

When I asked who had paid for my ticket, and how my room and board would be covered, the Imam brushed me off. An angel took care of it, Sis." So that's how at six months pregnant, and in the midst of a divorce, I was able to escape everything, and board a plane bound to a country I had been fantasizing about for most of my adult life. The trip would only be two weeks long, yet I knew it would be life changing.

I had a few weeks from the date of Imam Ibrahim's call to get ready for my trip. What would I pack for the trip of my dreams? What would I need. I decided to pack light. I would buy most of the things I wanted and needed while I was there. I took basic toiletries, my anti-nausea medication (just in case), my undergarments, and a few scarves. I would use my new allowance that had been awarded to buy clothes and shoes. I had seen many photos of the markets of Morocco, and I knew I could find everything I needed there.

It was with Allah's thanks and praise that I departed for the country I had read about and dreamed about for years. My heart was at ease as the plane prepared to take off. I suddenly knew that everything would be alright for me and my baby. I had faith that Allah would continue to provide for us. I had my *thikr* beads in one hand, and a small *dua* book in another. Yet the only *thikr* I could bring myself to say was *Alhamdulillah.*

To be Continued....

Made in the USA
Coppell, TX
27 February 2021